"You wouldn't be doing it for me," he emphasized. **"You'd be doing it for Mattio. What's a few weeks out of your life? The poor kid hasn't had much continuity in his so far."**

Even a compulsive liar had to speak the truth occasionally, Maya thought sardonically as her half sister's words floated through her head. *You don't know what Samuele is capable of.*

Well, she now knew one thing he was capable of after this breathtakingly blatant attempt to play on her feelings for Mattio.

"For future reference," she told him crisply, "I don't respond well to moral blackmail. Not that there will be—a future, I mean," she tacked on, wincing, because the only thing she'd managed to do was make it sound as though they had a past.

They didn't have a past, present or future.

It was just the entire off-the-scale hothouse weirdness of everything about the last few hours that had fed this strange feeling of intimacy, utterly misplaced intimacy, between them, she told herself.

Kim Lawrence lives on a farm in Anglesey with her university-lecturer husband, assorted pets who arrived as strays and never left, and sometimes one or both of her boomerang sons. When she's not writing, she loves to be outdoors gardening or walking on one of the beaches for which the island is famous—along with being the place where Prince William and Catherine made their first home!

Books by Kim Lawrence

Harlequin Presents

A Ring to Secure His Crown
The Greek's Ultimate Conquest
A Cinderella for the Desert King
A Wedding at the Italian's Demand
A Passionate Night with the Greek

Spanish Secret Heirs

The Spaniard's Surprise Love-Child
Claiming His Unknown Son

A Ring from a Billionaire

Waking Up in His Royal Bed

Visit the Author Profile page
at Harlequin.com for more titles.

Kim Lawrence

—

THE ITALIAN'S BRIDE ON PAPER

HARLEQUIN
PRESENTS

PRESENTS®

Recycling programs
for this product may
not exist in your area.

ISBN-13: 978-1-335-56808-3

The Italian's Bride on Paper

Copyright © 2021 by Kim Lawrence

All rights reserved. No part of this book may be used or reproduced in any manner whatsoever without written permission except in the case of brief quotations embodied in critical articles and reviews.

This is a work of fiction. Names, characters, places and incidents are either the product of the author's imagination or are used fictitiously. Any resemblance to actual persons, living or dead, businesses, companies, events or locales is entirely coincidental.

This edition published by arrangement with Harlequin Books S.A.

For questions and comments about the quality of this book, please contact us at CustomerService@Harlequin.com.

Harlequin Enterprises ULC
22 Adelaide St. West, 40th Floor
Toronto, Ontario M5H 4E3, Canada
www.Harlequin.com

Printed in U.S.A.

THE ITALIAN'S BRIDE
ON PAPER

PROLOGUE

Eighteen months previously, Zurich

MAYA AND BEATRICE had set out early, not alone, as the minibus ferrying tourists from the small ski resort to the airport in Zurich had been full of fellow travellers. They had all been stranded by the severe storm front that had resulted in the ski slopes being closed for the previous four days.

The storm was over now but *early* as a strategy had not worked—the minibus had been diverted before they'd even reached the terminal. The update texts the sisters had received so far from the airline had not been particularly encouraging or helpful and the details of the *airport security issue* mentioned in news reports remained worryingly vague.

There were rumours floating around on the Internet and also in the hotel bar situated within a short taxi drive of the airport where Maya and Beatrice had decided to wait out the delay.

They were not the only stranded travellers to take

this option; the place was full of easy-to-spot tense, grumpy and frustrated airline passengers, who were waiting to be given news.

'A response some time this side of Christmas would be good.' Beatrice's remark was not leavened with any of her normal humour. Her smooth brow was creased in a frown as she acquired a spare bar stool and sat down, arranging her long legs with casual elegance before turning her gaze back to the screen of her phone, as if willing their airline's promised update to appear.

'I might just go and check—'

'Fine,' Bea snapped, tight-lipped, without looking up.

Maya sighed. No sign of a full thaw just yet. They'd had the biggest row ever back at the ski resort, and, although they'd made up, the atmosphere was all a bit frigid. Some of the things her sister had said to her... Maya just couldn't get them out of her head; they kept playing on a loop.

'Really, Maya, relationship advice from *you*—what a joke! You've never even *had* a relationship. As soon as any half-decent guy gets within ten feet of you, you push him away,' Beatrice had said accusingly.

Maya had been stung. 'I dated Rob for months!'

'And you sabotaged that one just like all the others—and there have hardly been any others, have there? So *you've* never had your heart broken, for the simple fact that you won't take a risk—'

'*You* took a risk and look where it left you!' Maya had regretted the hasty words the moment they'd left her lips, and her swift efforts to de-escalate the situation had not exactly been a success. 'Sorry, Bea, but I hate to see you so unhappy. I know you chose to leave Dante, but he is clearly still messing with your—'

'Do not badmouth Dante to me...' her sister, who had spent the last few days doing just that herself, had growled back. 'Yes, I left him, Maya, but people do sometimes leave! And people die, we both know that too. It's called real life—and at least I have one.' Tears suddenly filled Beatrice's blue eyes. 'Sorry...I'm so sorry. I didn't mean that.'

After that final riposte, they had hugged and made up but Maya knew her sister had meant everything she'd said, and it was probably all true.

She considered saying something bright and cheery to lift the mood but decided that optimism would go down like a lead balloon. There was nothing she could say to make Beatrice feel any better, so it was probably better not to say anything at all.

She hitched in a little sigh and wished she'd remembered that saying nothing was an option last night. As she drifted away to stretch her legs, she threw the occasional glance over her shoulder at her sister, feeling the heavy weight of her total helplessness on her slender shoulders in the face of Beatrice's overwhelming unhappiness.

It was hard to watch someone you loved hurting.

She loved Beatrice, and no matter how often they squabbled or disagreed she knew that they had an unbreakable bond and that Beatrice would always be there for her.

The connection could not have been stronger if they had been biological sisters instead of Maya having been adopted by Beatrice's parents. Actually, Maya believed that it was stronger because she had a *real* sister out there and she had no connection with her. Her sister—actually, half-sister to be accurate—remained only a name and a face in a photo...*Violetta*. Her half-sister was clearly someone who, like their shared birth mother, apparently did not want to know Maya, did not want to be *embarrassed* by Maya's existence.

Searching out her birth mother was one of the few things she'd done that Maya had never shared with Beatrice or her adoptive mother, her *real* mother. When she had reached out to Olivia Ramsey, she had not been sure what to expect. And when the response had been an invitation to meet up for lunch, Maya had almost confided her very mixed feelings about the prospect of finally putting a face to the name of the stranger who had given her life and then immediately given her away. But she hadn't told Beatrice or their mother, and now eighteen months had passed, and so, she told herself, had the moment for sharing the secret.

Maya eased the vague sense of guilt she still felt for keeping that particular secret by convincing herself that this way there was no risk of Mum or Beatrice thinking that they were not enough of a family for her. Because they were her everything.

If she was being totally honest with herself, her re-

luctance to confide in them ran side by side with her
reluctance to relive in the telling Olivia Ramsey's rejection all over again. Once had been more than enough
to have it spelt out that the well-dressed, clearly well-
off woman who had given birth to you only wanted to
meet up with you years later to tell you, categorically,
that there was no place in her life for the daughter she
had given away. Showing Maya a photo of the daughter she *had* chosen to keep—Violetta—had been the
last nail in the coffin of Maya's hopes of building any
kind of relationship with her.

Maya couldn't remember exactly how she'd responded to Olivia's deliberately calm statements of
fact…something along the lines of, *No problem, but I'd
be grateful for any family medical history that might
be relevant to me,* which her birth mother, who had
not seemed overburdened with empathy, had accepted
at face value.

So she hadn't inherited her own empathy from her
biological mother—but what about her father? Well,
when she had finally worked herself up to asking
the question of his identity the answer hadn't left her
any the wiser. Apparently her mother hadn't known
his name—but he'd been good-looking, *very* good-
looking. Normally, Olivia had drawled, she didn't date
men under six feet.

The other woman had volunteered her reason for
giving Maya up without any prompting in the same
emotionally tone-deaf style: she'd admitted she would
almost *definitely* have kept Maya if her married

wealthy lover at the time had accepted her story that the baby was his. Only how was she to know he'd had a vasectomy? And surely Maya *had* to agree that saying you are single mother is a total turn-off for a real man?

'Ouch.'

The person wielding the trolley bag like a lethal weapon didn't even acknowledge the collision—of course they didn't, she thought darkly as she took refuge behind a potted palm. It turned out to be a perfect vantage point to watch the progress of an enterprising young artist who was based in the hotel foyer banging out a production line of cartoon portraits of new arrivals.

She rubbed her bruised shin and sighed. This last-minute skiing break had been doomed pretty much from the get-go; it had started badly and gone steadily downhill from there.

They had not even reached the chalet that had held so many good memories of long-ago childhood holidays when Maya had felt a migraine coming on.

It had definitely been a sign of things to come and proved, she reflected grimly, that it was a fatal mistake to try and recapture the past. But when the owner, an old family friend, had offered her and Beatrice the place for a song after a last-minute cancellation it had seemed too good an offer to pass up. So they'd eased their consciences by calling it a working holiday; after all, what better place, Beatrice had said, for Maya to get some inspiration for the winter collection she was trying to put together for the long-delayed launch of their fashion label.

But they had got very little actual work done, not due to Maya's migraine, or the lure of the ski slopes or even the après-ski fun, but solely thanks to the arrival of Beatrice's nearly ex-husband, Dante, who had turned up without the royal fanfare befitting his status as the Crown Prince of San Macizo and thrown her sister's life into chaos yet again.

Maya could forgive him for being the reason that their fashion label had not got off the ground first time around, but she couldn't forgive him for making her sister—who, until she'd fallen in love with Dante, had been the most optimistic and glass-half-full person Maya knew—so damned miserable. These days, even when Beatrice did smile, it was obviously an act; the shadow of misery visibly remained in her eyes.

From her vantage point beside the potted palm, Maya pushed away the thoughts of her sister's doomed marriage and watched in fascination as the young artist's hand moved across the paper managing in a few bold confident lines to pick out the essential features of his victims and magnifying them to comical proportions.

Maya had once thought she had artistic talent, but her youthful confidence in her ability had not withstood the campaign of mockery and humiliation waged by her stepfather.

The man was no longer in their lives and Maya had recovered most of the self-belief he had systematically destroyed, but never regained her uncomplicated joy of expressing herself in charcoal or paint.

In retrospect she could see that the dreadful Edward had probably unintentionally done her a favour—*goodness, but he'd hate to know that*—because there were so many artists far more talented than her who never made the grade and she didn't want to be one of the ranks of *nearly* good enough.

But this guy, she decided, was pretty good. Though to her amusement it was obvious that not everyone was happy with the frequently unflattering though always amusing portraits. But he was doing brisk business and he took the few knockbacks he received in his stride.

'Quantity over quality.' The youthful artist threw the comment towards her over his shoulder, making her start guiltily.

'I think you're very talented,' Maya said with a smile. She came out from behind the spiky palm fronds and moved in closer as the young man scrunched up his last rejected creation and attacked a fresh sheet.

'It pays the bills, or at least some of them, and beats starving in an attic. That is *so* last century or maybe the one before. God, not again!' He groaned as the hotel lights flickered and went out.

'Is it a power cut?' There had been a moment of total silence but now the place was filled with a jabber of voices, most saying much the same as she just had.

'Who knows? It's been doing it all morning. Ah, and now we have light.'

His clever hand was flying over the paper again, the

caricature coming to life like magic. With a few brief strokes a face began to appear along with, and this was the most magical part, a personality.

Head tilted, she studied the face that was taking form. A razor-sharp blade of a masterful nose made for looking down on the rest of humanity bisected a face with impossibly high cheekbones; a mouth with an overtly full, sensual upper lip contrasting with a firm, slightly cruel-looking lower, a deep chin cleft and a squared-off jaw that looked as though it were carved from granite completed the strikingly austere effect.

If the owner of those heavy-lidded eyes with exaggeratedly long curling eyelashes had in the flesh a fraction of the arrogance, self-belief and authority that was looking back at Maya from the paper, he was surely not going to be a potential customer of the artist.

In her private estimation, the subject of the cruel, clever portrait did not look like someone who could laugh at themselves.

Her warm dark brown eyes lifted, sparkling with amused speculative curiosity as she searched the room for the real-life inspiration, but the half-smile curling her lips quickly faded as she recognised the model for the unsolicited portrait.

It wasn't hard to spot him and that wasn't just because he stood inches above most people in the place. An imposingly tall, athletic figure in a long black wool trench coat that moulded to broad shoulders. His jet-black wavy hair was pushed back from a broad brow, nearly touching the snow-crusted collar of the coat as he moved through the press of bodies with a seemingly inbuilt exclusion zone. He was *not*, she mused, someone who could easily fade into the background.

Maya was conscious, not just of the uncomfortable in-your-face aura of alpha-male authority that he projected even from this distance, but the skin-tightening prickle of antagonism it produced in her. She chose to focus on that aspect while trying to ignore the pelvic flutter of awareness she felt as she watched him. He really was the living, breathing definition of compulsive viewing.

Love him or loathe him—there was no in between, she suspected. What was not in dispute was that there was something totally riveting about the man. Maya found herself both repelled and fascinated in equal measure, but then beauty always was fascinating—even if you were only trying to find a flaw in it—and he *was* pretty aesthetically pleasing!

The artist was good, but the closer his subject got, the more the limitations to his technique became apparent, though to be fair no amount of exaggeration could turn this subject into a joke. Everything about him, from the sense of restrained power in his panther-like fluid stride to his perfectly chiselled profile that combined strength and sensuality in equal measures, suggested he was *more* in every sense of the word.

The artist moving forward, sketch pad in hand to waylay his quarry, re-awoke Maya to her surroundings. She blinked and shook her head. The noise of the crowded space gradually filtering back, she was disturbed and embarrassed to realise just *how* hard she must have been staring at the man, as though she were... She lowered her eyes and felt the heat climbing to her cheeks as the mocking term *sex-starved* popped into her head.

It was not a description she could dispute in the literal sense, but the phrase somehow implied that the situation was a bad thing. Maybe it was for some people, but in her own personal situation celibacy was a conscious choice and not bad luck or, as Beatrice suggested, because she was frightened... She closed her eyes briefly, trying not to think about what Beatrice had said. Her sister was hurting badly, and was just lashing out.

Beatrice had passion, and Maya, well, she had... *caution*, and what she suspected was a pretty low sex drive, so she didn't envy poor Bea in the slightest.

She sometimes wondered if her sister had thought she had found with Dante the rare thing their parents had enjoyed before their father had been snatched away from them.

How would you even know if you found it? It seemed to Maya it was much more likely that—always supposing that special someone even existed in the first place—you would walk straight past your soulmate in the street. Maybe it was why most people, or so it seemed to her, either *settled* or, like Beatrice, imagined that they had found their soulmate, only to end up miserable and alone when things went wrong.

Or maybe Bea was right? Perhaps Maya was just

scared—scared of offering her love to a man only to have it rejected, or loving and losing him as Bea had… Pushing away the unhelpful thoughts before they could set up home in her head, she allowed herself to be further distracted by the advancing tall, powerful subject of the caricature.

No chance of mistaking him for a soulmate, she mused, rubbing her hands hard against her upper arms to ease the dark prickle she felt under her skin even through the layers, a sensation she had only previously experienced in the prelude to an electric storm.

She decided not to over-analyse this unexpected physical response to a total stranger, because though some people, her sister included, might suggest that *choice* was not involved where attraction was concerned, Maya firmly believed that you always had a choice. So as far as she was concerned, her head would always rule her heart and her hormones, not the other way around.

And there was also the purely practical side to consider. At this point in her life, romance or sex—*what was the difference?*—would have been a complication too far.

She and Bea were trying to start up a fashion business and one of them had to stay focused. Her sister was going through the trauma of a divorce and Maya needed to take up the slack. Her eyes slid briefly to where Bea sat, her death-ray stare glued to her phone, but Maya saw the sheer misery underneath the anger and her tender heart ached. Bea *really* wasn't the best advert for love right now, but, if it ever crept up on her, Maya was determined she was not going to allow her happiness to depend on a man—not *any* man.

She couldn't conceive of feeling that way, *ever*, she was not that person, but if a man made her unhappy there would be no looking back for her. She'd vowed to herself that she wouldn't be weighed down by someone else's baggage.

The heat, the crush of people, in here was unbearable and Samuele almost turned around and walked straight back through the revolving glass doors and into the street where the snow that was melting on his hair and overcoat had started to fall in earnest. But he had two hours to kill if his cautiously optimistic contact with inside information on the unfolding situation in the airport was to be believed, and suffering from hypothermia was not going to help the situation.

Was anything?

It deepened his sense of grinding frustration to know that there was a private flight ready for him on the runway—*so near and yet so far*—but waiting here remained his best bet of getting back to Rome in time to be with his brother before Cristiano went in for his scheduled surgery.

His fingers curled around the phone in his pocket as he thought about ringing Cristiano again, but on reflection he decided to wait until his revised travel plans were confirmed; he didn't want to make promises to his brother that he could not keep.

His facial muscles tightened in response to an explosion of laughter off to his right, and the sound of happiness grated on his nerve endings. He didn't want to hear it, he didn't want to be here, he wanted, no, he *needed* to be with his brother.

Cristiano was in the worst kind of trouble, trouble not of his making, and he was alone going through this ordeal, because the wife he adored had a *problem* with hospitals. Violetta did not do the *ugly* things in life, or, it seemed, *do* supporting the man she had married while someone cut into his brain to biopsy the reason for the blinding headaches and other assorted symptoms he had suffered in silence for the past six months.

'She cried when I told her,' Cristiano had said.

Female tears did not affect Samuele; well, not all female tears. Even now, after all these years, the memory of his mother's tears, mostly silent, still made his gut tighten in an echo of the remembered helplessness he had felt as a child. But tears that were purely cosmetic or used to manipulate left him cold, and Violetta's were both. Sadly, his brother was not as immune.

Samuele embraced the anger and contempt he felt towards Violetta even as it deepened the frown line that was threatening to become permanent between his thick slanted brows.

His hand came away wet as he dragged it across his dark hair, before clenching it into a fist. *Dio*, what was it with the men in his family and their bad choices in wives?

He supposed that he was just lucky he had never found the so-called *love of his life*. One thing was certain, if he ever saw her coming he'd sprint in the opposite direction. Samuele gave a thin cynical smile that left his dark eyes cold. He was reasonably confident he would not need his running shoes any time soon, because love was a complete work of fiction, and he was not living in the final scene of a Hollywood romantic comedy.

As he made his way over to the bar thoughts of what his brother was going through alone crowded in, dominating his thoughts, so it took a few seconds for the question being directed at him to penetrate.

Samuele glanced at the face of the young man, then looked down at the sketch being held out to him. He flinched inside. It was good, *too good*, for on the paper he saw a man who was clearly too unapproachable for even his own brother to confide in.

The anger he felt at himself, the frustration he felt at being unable first to save Cristiano from a toxic marriage and now from this disease that had sunk its claws into him, surged up inside him. The release after the past hours of enforced calm was volcanic, though it erupted not as fire but ice.

'Is that really the best you can do?' He allowed his blighting stare to rest on the caricature before he trained his hooded gaze back on the artist. 'The future is not looking bright for you, is it? I sincerely hope you have a plan B.' For a split second he felt a surge of satisfaction but then the kick of guilt came fast on its heels.

Talk about finding a soft target, he derided himself, contempt curling his lip, but this time it was aimed purely at himself. The only thing the guy had done was to be in the wrong place at the wrong time and to have a future for him to mock, unlike his brother, who might not.

Bleakness settled over him like a storm cloud, sucking away any form of hope.

'No problem.'

Instead of releasing the sketch to the young man who was backing away, Samuele held onto it, reaching in his pocket for his wallet with his free hand.

Always easier to throw money at a problem than say sorry, Samuele thought cynically, but before any conscience-easing exchange could be quietly made a small figure appeared, her dark hair a riot of flying Pre-Raphaelite curls, her sweater beneath a padded coat a flash of hot orange. She virtually flung herself between him and the young artist, who let go of his sketch and took a step back to avoid a collision.

She had moved so fast that Samuele had no idea where she had come from as she stood there, glaring up at him, her hands on the slim supple curves of her hips.

With a sinuous little spin that rather unexpectedly sent a slither of sexual heat through his body, she directed a warm look at the boy before turning sharply again and continuing to vibrate scorn towards Sam. 'He, *he* has more talent in his little finger than you… *you*…do in your whole body!'

She didn't raise her voice but every scathing syllable reached its intended target—him.

To say Samuele was taken aback by the sudden attack would have been an understatement. On another occasion he would have liked to have listened further to her voice, which, in contrast to her delicate build, was low and husky.

He could imagine it having a rich earthy tone, he could imagine it whispering private things for his ears only…which said a lot for his state of mind, considering that at that moment it shook with the emotions that were rolling off her—emotions that were neither warm nor intimate.

Samuele found his initial shock melting into something else equally intense, as enormous brown eyes flecked with angry golden lights narrowed on his face. The further kick of attraction he felt was suddenly so strong that the pain was actually physical as it settled hot in his groin. There were not many inches involved here—she did not even reach his shoulder—but every single one packed a *perfect* sensual punch.

She was so gorgeous that she couldn't have faded into the background if she'd tried, but she wasn't trying.

He really liked that.

He took in the details in one swift head-to-toe sweep. Her outfit appeared to be a glorious clash of colours; the only subdued element was her fur-cuffed snow boots, the velvet-looking close-fitting jeans tucked into them a deep rich burgundy, her sweater orange, the padded jacket that hung open turquoise.

She was either colour-blind or making a point; either way it worked, though, having reached her face again, he lost interest in colour coordination because the face occupied by those fire-spitting eyes was beautiful—heart-shaped, surrounded by long dark drifting tendrils of glossy hair that had not been confined in the messy topknot of curls pinned high on her head.

Her delicate bone structure and warm colouring conveyed a sense of both fragility and sensuality. The glowing flawlessness of her skin stretched across smooth, rounded high cheeks projected youth and vitality, the slight tilt of her neat nose gave it character and cuteness. Her mouth, however, was not cute at all; it was full and plump and at that moment pursed as she scowled at him.

He found his eyes lingering overlong on their pink softness, unaware that the hunger he was feeling was reflected in his hooded stare; he couldn't remember ever having experienced such an instant, intense visceral response to a woman before.

The way this man was looking at her... It was only her angry defiance that stopped Maya turning and running, letting him see that she was only brave on the outside.

If she was really brave it would not have crossed her mind even for a split second to remain a silent observer to this public display of cruel bullying, to pretend she hadn't seen.

The knowledge that she had been tempted to do just that made her almost as mad with herself as she was with the target of her wrath as her eyes were met and held by the piercing stare of the man in front of her, who was towering over her. She embraced her anger as well as the rush of blood to her head, only now she was experiencing another rush of blood, pounding all around her body, because the way he was looking at her made her feel totally exposed and shaky inside.

With a sharp blink of her eyes, she pushed back at the sensation of vulnerability, clenching her jaw as she gathered herself, deliberately focusing on what had triggered such an intense reaction.

As she opened her eyes again and met his stare head-on she was relieved that the *raw* expression she had just seen in his gaze was gone. She lifted her chin; she wasn't the kind of woman who melted into a puddle because a man looked as if he wanted her.

She focused instead on the soul-destroying contempt she had seen in his eyes as he'd spoken to the artist, the dismissive curl of his lips…every contemptuous syllable an eerie echo of ones she had heard so often from her stepfather. The situation had varied but the meaning was always the same: you are useless, worthless, don't even try.

She was no longer a child sitting there with her head bowed taking it, having her self-belief stripped away by her stepfather, and she wasn't about to watch it happen to someone else. She couldn't live with herself if she didn't call out that sort of bullying.

'Everyone's a critic,' she said hotly. 'Especially those who are incapable of understanding artistic talent. You wouldn't recognise quality if it bit you on the—' She felt her focus slipping away like wet rope through her fingers as one of the lights that had lagged behind the others suddenly burst back into life, shining like a stage spotlight directly at the object of her contempt. He was under the spotlight but *she* was the one who dried.

He sighed and stamped the last of the snow off his boots. 'This has not been the best of days for me.'

His voice was deep and edged with gravel, the slightest of accents only upping the fascination factor he held for her.

Her chin jerked upwards. 'Is that a *threat*?'

'How much?' He tossed the question to the youth over her head.

'You think you can buy your way out of anything, I suppose,' she muttered bitterly. Everything about him screamed money and exclusivity, she decided, as her glance lingered on the breadth of his shoulders.

But the realisation that anger was no longer solely responsible for the dizzying adrenaline rush coursing through her body hit her.

He was objectionable and a bully, but she was ashamed to admit she was a long way from being immune to the waves of male magnetism he exuded.

Taking a deep sustaining breath, she broke the spell of those eyes and felt a trickle of moisture snake down her back. She was *not* about to fall in lust with some random stranger. 'You have talent.' She threw the words over her shoulder at the artist. 'And *you*,' she added, killing her smile, 'won't destroy anyone's confidence or fill them with self-doubt.' She lifted her chin a defiant notch and thought, *Not on my watch!*

Samuele had been on the receiving end of a few un-friendly looks in his time, but nothing that came close to the sheer loathing that he was being regarded with by this total stranger.

He found himself wondering what it would take to make her smile at him... *Possibly seeing you lying dead at her feet*, suggested the sarcastic voice in his head.

'And never,' she ground out through clenched pearly teeth to the young man, 'let *anyone* tell you otherwise.'

'I'm fine—' began the artist.

She cut across him unapologetically. 'Never apolo-gise for someone else's rudeness, and don't let *anyone* gaslight you. You have to believe in yourself.'

Samuele was caught between annoyance and amusement. She clearly had issues, but they were none of his business. 'What are you, his girlfriend or his life coach?'

'Just someone who doesn't like bullies,' she sneered. 'What do you do for an encore, show kittens who's boss?' She widened her eyes in mock admiration. 'A big tough man like you, what inadequacy are you compensating for?' she wondered. 'Dumped by the girlfriend?'

'Wondering if there's a vacancy?' he shot back.

He couldn't help his satisfaction as she flushed bright red. 'In your dreams.'

'Oh, I have very interesting dreams,' he drawled in a voice like warm honey.

'I am not interested in your dreams, thank you,' she retorted haughtily. 'Or your suggestive comments.'

The lights went out again with no warning flicker and in the blackness there was the sound of a glass breaking and several giggles and shouts.

In the darkness Maya felt a whisper of sensation on her lips, light as a butterfly's wings. She sighed and shivered, and began to stretch upwards towards the touch, but just as suddenly it was gone, making her wonder if she'd imagined it.

The lights came back on.

He'd disappeared.

She blinked as the young artist handed her the sketch he had done with an admiring look. 'Man, you are fierce!'

'You bet you she is!'

It was Beatrice who'd rushed over and enfolded her in a hug. 'I am so, so sorry what I said before. I know you were only trying to help me and I was a monster.'

'No...no...'

'Utter and total. Really, Maya, I think you have it right; you never want to feel as rotten as this. So, who was that hunk you were just yelling at?'

'I have no idea.'

CHAPTER ONE

MAYA PUT DOWN the phone and eased her bottom on the edge of the table where she had perched for the duration of the call. She pushed a section of hair that had escaped her casual topknot back from her face with her forearm and yawned. If she hadn't been waiting for the call she would have already been in bed, which, given it was a Friday night, she was twenty-six, single and living in London, probably made her what most people would call sad.

She knew she was going to have to do something about her social life, or rather the lack of it, although the irony was she'd actually had an invite tonight: a group from work had been going out for cocktails to celebrate someone's engagement. She had had to refuse, explaining her mum was travelling overseas to stay with her sister and had promised to contact her the moment she arrived.

'A long trip?' someone had asked.

'San Macizo.'

She didn't have to elaborate further. The exotic

island had been the location of a recent blockbuster movie and had been very much in the news, as well as the subject of numerous articles. Like the articles the conversation had swiftly moved on from the stunning scenery to Maya's brother-in-law, with his film-star looks, bemoaning the fact that the hot heir to the throne of San Macizo, the delicious Dante, was no longer available; he'd married an English girl, who everyone wanted to be.

If Maya had contributed to this part of the conversation she could have explained that the English girl was her own sister Beatrice, who, after being reconciled with her husband, had now happily taken on the role of Princess and mother, making both roles her own.

Bea was pregnant again and suffering severe morning sickness, so Maya was glad their mum was there to offer support and also fuss over her delicious little granddaughter, Maya's goddaughter.

But Maya had stayed quiet, not because she wasn't proud of her royal connection, but because it was easy to predict the questions they might have asked, like, *If your sister's a princess, how come you're working as a window dresser for a department store?*

The answer, according to her sister, was that Maya was too damned proud, stubborn and stupid to take help when it was freely offered to her. Maya had really appreciated the offers of help, and she knew they were well meant and sincere, but, though it might take longer, when she finally got to where she wanted to be, it would mean so much more to know she had done it herself and not just used her connections and their bank balance.

She yawned, easing one fluffy mule back on her narrow foot, and caught herself thinking about making a mug of cocoa… *Oh, God…cocoa…get a life, Maya!* Would the wine she had opened last weekend still be drinkable?

Cocoa or last week's wine? She had not completely decided when the doorbell rang.

This time of night the only person who rang her doorbell was the pizza delivery service and she had definitely not ordered one.

Puzzled but not alarmed, she went to the door.

She tightened the belt on her robe before she opened the door a crack—one of these days she really would get a safety chain.

It was not a pizza, it was a woman, and she was not alone. Before becoming a proud aunt, Maya wouldn't have been able to guess the age of the dark-haired baby the woman carried, but if asked now she would have estimated him at somewhere between three and four months. But she wasn't in any state to guess; behind the flickering of her silky, sooty dark lashes, the eyes they framed were blank with shock as she stared at her visitors.

She hardly noticed the door swinging wide as she took a tiny step back, but finally she breathed out a shakily incredulous, 'V…Violetta…?'

Because although it really *couldn't* be, the woman standing there—tall, slim, looking as though she

had just stepped out of the pages of a fashion maga-
zine, her river-straight waist-length hair with a mirror
gloss, her make-up perfectly highlighting her china-
blue eyes—was the same woman she had seen in the
photo her birth mother had proudly shown her—her
half-sister. Maya still had it—it was the only thing her
birth mother had ever given her.

'You're Mia?'

'Maya.'

'Of course, Mummy described you perfectly...but
I'd have known you anywhere!'

'You would?'

'Absolutely! There's just this *connection* between
us; I can feel it, my little sister. Can't you?' As she bent
forward to kiss the air either side of Maya's face, Maya
instinctively leaned back, not to avoid contact, but to
stop the baby being sandwiched between them. 'Although you're older than me, aren't you? But I'm sure
you look lovely with some make-up on.'

Maya blinked rapidly, unnerved by Violetta's rather
Siamese cat stare and too utterly confused to even
register the implication that she clearly did not look
lovely without it.

'No...yes, that is, I'm...' Maya shook her head.
'You...here...' She took a deep breath and focused on
forming an entire sentence. 'Just what is happening?'

'I needed help—' Maya watched with horror as her
half-sister's slender shoulders began to shake, and her
lovely face crumpled as tears began to roll in slow motion down her cheeks.

Maya's wary antagonism melted into genuine concern. 'Is there anything I can do?'

'I shouldn't be here, really… I'm so sorry. I should have rung you, I know, but I was afraid you'd say no and I had nowhere else to go. You're our *only* hope, so please don't send us away,' she begged plaintively, hugging the sleepy baby so tight that he gave a little cry of protest.

It jolted Maya free of her shock. 'Oh, no…no, of course not—' She broke off at the sound of heavy breathing a moment before a figure carrying luggage under both arms came into view.

'There's no lift, and you don't travel light.'

Maya, who was feeling as though events were getting way ahead of her, took in the numerous bags now filling the doorway and the panting, sweaty-faced new arrival, who did not look happy, though his frown vanished when Violetta looked at him with tears shimmering in her beautiful eyes.

'Oh, you poor thing! Mia was just about to help you, weren't you?' she assured him, an emotional hitch in her voice as she turned to Maya. 'This man—George, isn't it?—has been a total angel… Now, where is my purse…? Oh, Mia, would you get it for me? And don't forget to give George a healthy tip.'

Mia? Ah, well, she'd been called worse, and she had other priorities, like locating her purse, paying the driver and dragging the luggage wedged in the doorway inside. By the time she had accomplished these tasks Violetta and the baby had transferred themselves to the sofa in her living room, and while the baby dribbled and chewed his fist his mother was giving her attention to the interior decor. It was patently obvious from the flare of her nostrils that shabby chic was not her thing.

Maya waited. There were just so many things to say she didn't know where to start, though it seemed she didn't need to.

Her visitor whispered a tremulous, 'I'm sorry.'

'For what?'

The literal response drew a tiny frown and the intense blue gaze narrowed calculatingly on Maya's face. 'Turning up without warning this way…but I was desperate, although I swear I've wanted to reach out to you for so long…'

'You have? But I thought your mother… *Olivia* said that neither of you wanted anything to do with me…' Maya bit her lip, hating that telltale quivering of her voice.

'When Mummy met you, I was…*vulnerable*. It's a time in my life that I still struggle to talk about. And Mummy always was…*is* very protective of me. Later on, I must admit I was afraid that you'd resent me, even though—' Her lips quivered this time, and her voice cracked. 'Even though Cristiano said that I should… I'm sorry—'

She looked around helplessly until Maya located a box of tissues on the desk behind her. The practical gesture seemed pretty inadequate given the situation, but it was better than nothing.

'Cristiano?'

'My husband.' Violetta took a tissue and dabbed it gently to her miraculously smooth and unblotchy cheek. Maya couldn't believe there wasn't even a smudge to her make-up. 'But he died without ever seeing our dearest Mattio.'

Maya's wide, shocked eyes went to the little baby— her nephew!—and her heart ached for him and his mother. How on earth did someone recover from a tragedy like that?

'I am so sorry to hear that.'

The baby chose that moment to grab a strand of his mother's dramatically coloured hair in his chubby fist. Violetta let out a squeal, her expression of tragic suffering suddenly morphing into annoyance.

'Let me.' Maya leaned forward and unwound the tiny yet tenacious fingers from the glossy strand that started auburn at the root and went through an extraordinary range of shades ending in a deep strawberry blonde at the tip. It was hard, given the artistry, to guess what her natural hair colour was.

'And now I…I have nothing!'

Struggling to respond with anything that didn't sound lame and shallow, Maya offered another tissue, which was refused as her half-sister shook back her glossy hair.

'You have this little one and he has you,' Maya finally said hoarsely as she felt her throat thicken with tears. She swallowed hard; if *she* started crying it would not be as pretty as Violetta's efforts. 'All a child needs is to be wanted and loved,' she added, even as she reminded herself that love did not pay the bills. 'I know it must be hard financially being a single parent and—'

'But Mattio is an Agosti!'

Maya shook her head, confused.

Her ignorance appeared to shock the younger woman, whose blue eyes flew wide. 'He is heir to half the Agosti fortune.'

'Oh, right...' Maya nodded vaguely, getting the picture, though to her mind, as useful as silver spoons might be, surely a child would be better off with a living father?

'Of course, the money should have come to me as his widow, but Cristiano changed his will, and I know exactly who to blame for that,' she said darkly. 'Not that I have a problem with the money going to Mattio,' she added hastily, seeing the look on Maya's face.

Maya nodded, feeling uncharitable that she had trouble believing this claim. How could she blame the woman? It must be hard if she had expected to inherit.

'I have a problem with having to go to *Samuele* for every penny. *He* saw to it that Cristiano left financial control of our child's fortune to him.'

'Who is Samuele?' Maya asked, seriously struggling to keep up.

'He is Cristiano's older brother. He's always hated me—he was jealous because Cristiano stopped letting him make all the decisions. Oh, I don't blame my darling Cristiano, he was vulnerable and Samuele dripped poison in his ear and turned my own husband against me... I can tell you don't believe me, but then no one does!' she cried, her voice rising to a shrill hopeless note. 'They don't understand—they think that Samuele is caring of his family, including me.'

Maya pressed her fingers to the throbbing in her temples. With each word a picture appeared that was horribly familiar to her, channelling her anger into a quiet resolve.

'Oh, I understand. I understand *perfectly*,' she said, 'how someone can appear one thing on the surface and be something very different.'

Before he had married her and Beatrice's mother, Maya had believed her stepfather was the person that the world thought he was: caring and considerate and, most importantly, making her grieving mother happy again. Then they had married and the abuse had begun, so subtle, so insidious that her mother hadn't seen that she was being isolated from her friends, her support network, and in the end even her daughters, until it was almost too late. Maya had not known then but she did realise now that Edward had seen her own closeness to her mother as an obstacle to his all-consuming need for total control over his wife.

Golden girl, he had mocked as he'd deliberately set about revealing to the world and her mother that she was not golden at all; she was useless, she was deceitful.

'They call it coercive control,' Maya said grimly. 'But you're not alone.' And neither had she been; Beatrice had been there for her. Now it was Maya's turn to offer support to another woman and she was glad to be able to.

'You understand!' Gratitude shone in her half-sister's eyes that was quickly replaced by despair. 'But there's nothing you can do to help me, because he has everything. Samuele has money and power, and now I think…' She faltered, kissing the top of her baby's head before revealing, 'No, I *know* he's trying to take my baby away from me, but no one will believe me. But maybe they are right?' she cried wildly.

'No, don't believe that, ever! Believe in yourself,' Maya replied fiercely, her voice shaking with emotional emphasis.

'Coming here was a total act of impulse. It all became too much for me and…well, I just need some space to work out what to do next.'

'You can stay here with me. Take all the time you need.'

'Really?'

What are you letting yourself in for?

Immediately ashamed of the momentary flicker of uncertainty, Maya lifted her chin and she smiled. 'Really.'

It had been the early hours of the morning before Maya had finally crawled into bed, but despite being exhausted she slept in fits and starts, repeatedly waking and remembering all over again that Beatrice's room was not empty any more. It was occupied by a half-sister she did not really know, a half-sister whom, given what she was going through, Maya *ought* to feel a connection with, and she was confused by the fact she didn't.

But then maybe it was unrealistic to expect emotions like that to just materialise out of thin air, and it obviously didn't help that she found herself comparing Violetta to Beatrice and finding her blood relative coming out second.

Whatever she did not feel for Violetta was more than compensated for by what she *did* feel for Mattio. She had felt nervous when Violetta, pleading utter exhaustion, had handed over the baby to Maya to feed and change.

Maya had been surprised by the little ache in her heart when she had eventually handed him back, and it had made her wonder if her own birth mother had felt that way when Olivia had given her up? Had the sound of her crying triggered the same instinct that had Maya leaving her warm duvet cocoon as she heard Mattio wailing in the next room? Dragging both hands in a futile smoothing motion across her wildly tumbled dark curls, she swung her feet to the floor.

Maya closed down the useless speculation over her birth mother and caught sight of herself in the mirror as she grabbed a robe off the hook behind the door, the sleep-deprived face that stared back at her bringing a fleeting grimace to her face.

On the plus side, her disturbed night had not been troubled by the recurrent dream that she half dreaded, half longed for. She never remembered specific details. On waking all that remained was an erotic blur; the sense of deep yearning, the memory of a deep honeyed voice and a strong sense of shame that usually lingered until she'd had her second cup of coffee.

It hardly seemed possible that a chance encounter so many months ago with a tall, arrogant stranger should leave such a strong imprint on her unconscious. She lifted a hand to her suddenly tingling lips. Had he kissed her or had that been a fiction invented by her overactive imagination too?

An extra loud baby cry had her shrugging off the memory of temperature-raising dark eyes. Once outside her room, she thought she could hear the distressed baby cries even more loudly, but then her experience of crying babies was not what anyone would call extensive.

Her niece probably *did* cry, but whenever Maya saw her, which was too infrequently, little Sabina Ella, a deeply contented child, always seemed to be smiling or examining the world around her with big solemn enquiring eyes or giving the deep little belly chuckle that was impossible not to react to.

There was a wistful element to the small smile that played across the fullness of Maya's soft mouth in response to the memories of her last visit to San Macizo. She was really glad her sister had found the happiness she deserved, and that she was finally reconciled with her husband, but she couldn't help wishing that

Beatrice had found all those elements a little closer to home.

Approaching the bedroom door, she paused and after a moment knocked, raising her voice to make herself heard above the distressed bawling inside.

'Is there anything I can do or get for you, Violetta?' she asked, directing her question to the closed door. She paused again and waited, head tipped to one side in a listening attitude, but the only thing she heard was Mattio.

Pitching her voice louder, she repeated her question and was not really surprised when there was still no response; she could barely hear herself above the crying. Tapping on the door again, she called out the other woman's name several times to give her some warning as she pushed it slowly open.

'Violetta?' Maya scanned the room, empty but for the travel cot that held the baby, his wailing subsiding into a series of gulping, heartbreaking breathy sobs as he heard her voice.

Maya walked across to the cot and whispered a tentative, 'Hello there.' The baby's face was red, his eyes puffy with prolonged crying, and when he saw Maya he didn't quiet completely but he did stretch out his chubby little hands towards her.

Maya felt something tighten in her chest, the strangest sensation.

'Oh…' She swallowed, feeling the unexpected heat of tears pressing against her eyelids. That's all we need, more tears, she told herself sternly as she blinked hard.

'So where is your mummy?' she asked, refusing to think about the significance of the undisturbed decorative pillows on the bed until she actually had to. 'Violetta!'

The baby, clearly objecting to her raised voice, started crying in earnest again.

'No...no, don't do that! I'm sorry, don't...oh, God!' Taking a deep breath, she leaned into the cot and lifted out the warm, damp baby. 'Righto!' she said, channelling slightly desperate cheer as she settled him awkwardly against her hip. 'So, let's go find your mummy, shall we?'

The knot of panic in her chest had expanded to the size of a heart-compressing boulder as, jiggling the baby in her arms, she walked through every room in the flat. It didn't take long—there was nowhere a cat could hide, let alone a person—but she retraced her steps anyway.

'This is not happening,' she muttered. But it was, and she had to deal with it. 'Don't worry, it'll be fine,' she said to the baby, and saw that his little head was propped on her shoulder. He had fallen asleep, exhausted by his crying.

There had to be a perfectly logical explanation for this, she thought, and then spotted the note propped behind a framed photo of Beatrice with Dante, who was looking at his wife with an expression of total adoration. There was a name scrawled across the front of the envelope.

Not her own name, but *Mia*.

Well, some people were just bad with names. Weren't they?

She stared at the envelope with a sudden sick feeling of dread in the pit of her stomach. Probably, given the situation, it was totally justified.

Why prolong it, just do it! Better to know the worst.

Or was it, was it really? There were occasions when blissful ignorance had a definite appeal and Maya had always struggled with the 'rip the plaster off and get the pain over with' mindset.

One arm supporting the sleeping baby, she glanced down at his sweet, tear-stained face and wished she could copy him. She blew out a gusty breath and decided to put him back in his cot.

Baby settled, the next thing on her checklist—because this wasn't about delaying, it was prioritising—was the formula sitting in the fridge to inspect. While the letter wasn't going anywhere, when he woke Mattio would need feeding and, of course, changing. Locating the changing mat and nappies and clean clothes took another few minutes, but the letter was still sitting there and now she had run out of more important and less potentially explosive things to do.

With a hiss of exasperation, she snatched at it and ripped it open, but she had barely scanned the contents when the doorbell rang, making her jump.

Samuele lifted his hand off the doorbell and applied his clenched fist to the wooden panel, fighting the urge to batter his way through the last barrier between him and his nephew.

Instead, he took a deep breath and reminded himself that, while Violetta was a piece of work, selfish, cold and manipulative, she would not harm her own child. This small soothing piece of positivity didn't lower his levels of frustration because, though it might be true, Samuele also knew that she would not hesitate to use Mattio to further her own agenda. This particular vengeful widow had never put anyone's needs above her own self-interest and motherhood had not altered that aspect of her one iota.

Samuele's hand lifted to the fading red line that ran down from his cheekbone to his jaw, glad that the one on the other side had already gone. *He* was the target of Violetta's spite, not the baby, but that didn't mean the innocent child could not be collateral damage. His gut tightened with guilt that he had not seen this, or something like it, coming.

He had promised Cristiano so easily that he would take care of his child. Pulling himself up to his full height, he fixed his steely gaze on the door. He would make good on that promise.

He heard the sound of a key in the lock and took a step back—waiting for…who?

The words of the note still echoing in her head, Maya's unsteady hands were shaking so hard she struggled to get a good grasp on the key in the lock, not realising until a lot of fumbling later that it wasn't locked, it couldn't be locked, because Violetta had left it open when she left.

Just thinking of how *desperate* Violetta must have felt to leave her own baby with a virtual stranger sent a fresh surge of emotion through her body. She'd said in the brief note that she would come back for Mattio… and she *would*, Maya was sure of that. Perhaps she already had?

Relief that Violetta had realised she couldn't desert her baby washed over Maya in a heart-steadying wave. She gave the stiff door an enthusiastic tug, stepping forward as it swung open to reveal, not her half-sister, but a shockingly familiar imposing figure. The welcoming smile of relief vanished from her eyes as reality collided with her dreams.

Her voice shook with the sheer impact of recognition that nailed her to the spot, leaving her feeling as though she had just run full pelt into a wall.

The seconds ticked away as two sets of eyes locked. It was Maya who finally broke the tableau, her chest heaving as she gasped for air before giving voice to her unedited reaction at being faced with the person who had unlocked something inside her so many months ago that she still refused to acknowledge.

'Oh, no… *You!*'

No matter how many times you skydived, there was always that moment of shock in the split second when you actually launched yourself into space. This was the first time Samuele had experienced that same sensation with both his feet still on the ground.

His hooded gaze moved in a slow sweep upwards from her bare feet to the top of her glossy head, taking in everything in between. He clenched his teeth, the twist of lust in his belly that crossed the border into pain all too familiar.

His reaction to this woman was just as visceral as it had been the first time, when her liquid dark eyes had flashed fire at him for being rude to that artist. The same eyes now were glazed with shock. His glance lingered on the soft full outline of her mouth… He had thought about that mouth a lot since that day, wished he had followed through with his instinct and actually kissed her, so he'd know what she tasted like.

A muscle clenched in his jaw. '*You* are the *sister*?' And presumably a part of Violetta's plan to extort money from him.

Not ready to admit to anything just yet, Maya countered this accusation with her own question.

'*You're* the *brother-in-law*?' The man in her dreams, the man she had met for only moments eighteen months ago, and yet who had imprinted himself indelibly inside her head, was Violetta's persecutor!

One dark brow arched upwards as with a contemptuous curl of his lips he announced, 'I am Samuele Agosti, and, as I'm sure you know, I am here to return my nephew home to Italy.'

He had lost none of the arrogance she remembered

from Zurich, and, unfortunately for her, none of his rampant maleness. She folded her arms protectively across her chest.

'Well, you've had a wasted journey.'

'Where is she?'

The question was not directed at her but past her, unlike the fleeting scornful glance that she was definitely the intended recipient of.

Her chin went up. 'I'd like you to leave now.' The door only moved a couple of inches before it met the immovable obstacle of his size-twelve foot shod in handmade leather. 'Home for a child is where his mother is—' Maya stopped, unable to prevent the self-conscious dismay from spreading across her face as she realised that even if this were true, Mattio's mother wasn't here.

She was the only thing standing between this man and her baby nephew.

'You don't sound too sure about that,' he remarked.

'You know what I *am* sure of—that I'm going to call the police if you don't leave in the next ten seconds.'

'The thing about threats is that you have to be willing to follow through with them, or at least convince the person they're directed at that you are.'

Maya found her eyes following the motion of his long fingers as they moved from the open-necked collar of his white linen shirt and the vee of olive skin at the base of his throat, up his neck and across the dusting of dark stubble on his firm, square jaw.

There was a challenge in his smile, and the male

aura he radiated—his *presence*—could fill an entire arena. This was not an arena, it was a very small, unglamorous hallway, and it made her feel very small and insignificant.

The recognition of the feeling made her square her shoulders. She didn't care who he was, this was *her* space! She drew herself up to her full diminutive height, managing to project a sense of confidence, which was a miracle in itself, considering she was not dressed for dignity—a fact that was just hitting home to her.

Without taking her eyes off his face, she casually reached for the tie on her robe and knotted it around her middle before smoothing down her hair, but it was a pointless exercise, she knew, so she gave it up. Dignity was more than skin-deep.

'I don't bluff.' She tightened her belt another vicious notch and pushed out abruptly, 'Just go away.'

CHAPTER TWO

'WHERE IS SHE?'

The question flustered her and put her on the defensive.

'She who?'

This drawn-out innocent act tried his temper, but not as much as the unwelcome recognition of his own initial shock reaction to the sight of the woman barring his way. God alone knew how long he had stood there literally in the grip of a hormonal rush worthy of a teenager.

Or a man who had gone too long without?

He found the latter explanation far more palatable and very easily solved. Sex was like any other hunger. It was not at all complicated as long as you didn't start imagining there was anything other than a mutual attraction there. No matter how strong, no lust had a shelf life beyond a few weeks.

'I think we should take this inside, don't you?'

Sam swallowed as an image of her wide dilated eyes and messy hair floated through his head. Just how responsive would she be in bed...? Frowning in response to the sly voice of his libido, he pushed the images away to focus on the reason he was here.

She panicked. 'No!'

Her response was so unexpected it stopped him and his thought processes dead in their tracks, and it took him a few moments to actually take on board what she was doing.

She stood there stubbornly, a hand braced against either side of the door frame.

'I *don't* think we should take this inside,' she said firmly.

'You've got to be joking,' he said, feeling an unexpected stab of admiration as she tightened her grip on the door frame, blocking his way with, what, an entire seven stone nothing?

Stronger than his admiration was the mental image of placing his hands around her ribcage and bodily removing her from his path. His thought lingered on the image long enough to count as self-indulgent and he frowned slightly.

Maya compressed her lips and maintained her defiant stance even though, truthfully, she was starting to feel a little foolish. As gestures went this one was pretty futile, and she was still suffering from the weird feeling of having entered a conversation midway through.

Forget about the why, and the how, just focus on the now, she told herself, and in the now she physically represented no obstacle to him. He could have lifted her out of the way with one hand tied behind his back... It was far more worrying that the idea of him doing that made her breath come a little too fast as, under the protective cover of her lashes, she made a co-vert scan of his long lean length. It only revealed what she already knew: he had the physique of a Greek god who worked out a lot—or in this case an Italian god.

So nothing has changed in the twenty seconds since you last drooled over him, Maya!

'Violetta!' He pitched his deep voice to carry and Maya groaned.

'All right,' she sighed out. It was easier to admit the truth, or at least this portion of it, than have him wake Mattio. Dealing with one Agosti male at a time was enough and this one was way too big to rock to sleep. She cleared her throat and pushed away a deeply distracting image of his dark head on her breast. 'She isn't here, but—'

'And Mattio?'

'Well, you can't have him...because he's not here either.'

Sam's brows lifted at her obviously panicky tack-on. 'You are a very bad liar,' he observed, unaccountably disgruntled at the discovery. 'Look, enough.' He brought one long-fingered brown hand down in a slash-ing motion. 'I really don't care who you have in there, beyond my nephew, who belongs with me.'

'I don't have anyone in there!' she retorted.

But in his mind's eye, Samuele was seeing a lover

sleeping in her bed. Grimly, he found he had no problem disturbing this exhausted, sleeping boyfriend.

'You always walk around dressed like that after
midday?'

Catching his drift, Maya blushed. 'My sex life is
none of your business,' she countered, thinking, *It's
just as well he doesn't know I haven't got one.*

Life might be interesting if it were his business.

As he veiled his eyes with his ludicrously long
lashes she glimpsed a gleam before he delivered a flat
statement that came out sounding a lot like a threat.

'I can stay here all day.'

'No, you *really* can't.'

'I—' He stopped at the unmistakable sound of a
baby cry.

'Oh, my God, look what you've done now!' she exclaimed.

On the receiving end of a 'rot in hell' glare, he did
not immediately respond to the opening as she stood
there, hands pressed together as though she were praying.

A moment later she breathed out. 'I think he's gone
back to sleep.'

'I am not going away without Mattio.'

There was no hint of concession in his voice or on
his chiselled features. Thinking hard, she considered
his beautiful fallen-angel face, her eyes drifting over
the angular contours of his lower jaw and hollowed
cheeks, which were dusted with dark stubble that em-

phasised the razor edge of his carved cheekbones and the sensual curve of his upper lip.

'So, I think this is where you invite me in.'

'Or what, you'll barge your way in? I'm warning you, I really will call the police.'

He lifted his eyes from where they had drifted to the gaping neckline of her silky nightshirt, and she couldn't help the shiver of excitement that sizzled down her spine.

'Feel free if Violetta actually isn't here.' He subjected her face to a speculative laser-like scan. 'I'm quite sure this situation will be of interest to them.'

It suddenly occurred to her that this might well be the case. She weighed her options and discovered she didn't have many.

With a tight-lipped sigh she stepped to one side and without another word he shouldered his way past her.

'Come in, why don't you?' she drawled, sarcasm masking her apprehension as she glared at the man who now dominated her small living room.

Samuele scanned the modest space that had probably been dominated by the stacks of books and a dressmaking dummy draped with fabric, only now they took second place to a baby buggy, a stack of disposable nappies and general baby detritus. But the item his eyes zeroed in on was a stuffed rabbit. He felt his throat thicken, remembering when it had been new, his brother's way of telling him that he was going to be an uncle.

'Don't you mean you're going to be a father?' Samuele had responded.

'Maybe.' His brother had handed him the toy. 'The
cancer's back, Sam. I start chemo next week. So, you
see, this kid is going to need you to be around.'

'You'll be around for them! You beat it once, you'll
beat it again.'

'Sure, I will.'

They had kept up the pretence, dancing around the
truth, right up until the last minute. Sometimes he
thought that his little brother had been protecting him,
rather than the other way around.

Maya watched a muscle jump in his cheek as he bent
forward, pausing before he straightened up with a soft
toy in his hand. For a split second she saw something
in his face that made him seem almost vulnerable. She
experienced a troubling moment of what felt scarily
like empathy, but then he looked at her, and his eyes
were not those of a man who needed her empathy, they
were hard and cold and ruthless.

'So where is Violetta hiding?'

'She's not hiding anywhere…' Unable to sustain
eye contact with the darkness in his, she transferred
her gaze to the toy trailing from his fingers. 'She's…
gone out.'

'Where and when will she be back?' he asked as he
arranged himself in the nearest chair.

Maya struggled to contain her panic as she watched
him stretch his long legs out in front of him. 'I don't

exactly know,' she said, pretty sure she was sounding as lame as she was feeling.

His eyes narrowed. 'Don't know exactly what—where or when?'

'All of those.'

'You know very little,' he observed unpleasantly.

'I know you are sitting in my chair and I didn't invite you in… I'm sure that's against the law.'

He grinned. 'Only if I'm a vampire.'

Her lips tightened at the flippancy but she couldn't help thinking that it wouldn't actually be such a stretch to see him in the role of a sexy vampire!

'Look, this is ridiculous.' *So was imagining offering him your neck.*

Ridiculous would be him allowing himself to be fobbed off. 'I'll wait for her.'

'No!' She gulped and added, 'I'm expecting some—' She broke off as the sound of a low murmur amplified by the baby monitor on the coffee table filled the room. 'Oh, God, he's woken up again.'

Her eyes widened as her uninvited visitor vaulted to his feet in one smooth stomach-clenching action. Maya was only a heartbeat away from throwing herself physically in his path as he approached the door leading to Beatrice's bedroom. It was crazy; she still thought of it that way, even though her sister had only spent a few nights there before her life had taken a very different direction.

What would Bea do?

She wouldn't have let him in.

Get a grip! Beatrice wasn't here, she was, and she couldn't let Beatrice fight her battles any more. Maya was never going to give in to a bully, not ever again.

She got between him and the bedroom door, and she turned to face the advancing figure, who suddenly seemed about ten feet tall, raising her hands as if she could actually physically stop him. She knew she'd have had more chance of stopping a hurricane! It struck her that the analogy was very apt—there was something truly elemental about him.

'There are rules,' she said, refusing to give ground. 'Ground rules.'

He looked astonished. *'Rules...?'*

'If Mattio has fallen asleep again, don't wake him up—please.'

She held her breath, once again seeing in her head the image of herself being lifted bodily by two strong hands—which produced another worryingly ambiguous reaction low in her stomach.

She cleared her throat. 'It took a long time for him to settle.'

Sam looked from the door to her pleading face and after a moment he nodded.

Her relief seemed genuine. 'So, what is Violetta playing at? What little scheme have you two been hatching?' he asked.

'I hate to ruin a conspiracy theory with inconvenient things like facts, but there is no scheme or hatching, there is no *us two*.'

'She is your sister, isn't she?' The fact that she

looked sexily wholesome on the surface made her far more dangerous than her overtly glamorous but entirely toxic sister.

'Half-sister, actually.'

'She ran to you, left her baby with you, so you two must be close.'

A little laugh escaped Maya's parted lips. 'I hadn't even met her before last night when she turned up with Mattio.'

Unlikely as it sounded, Samuele found he was inclined to believe the ring of truth in her voice.

'So she's using you. Typical.'

'No, she's not... Do not twist everything I say.'

'So when did she leave?'

There seemed very little to gain from not telling him. 'I'm not sure. I woke up, and there was a note...' Maya's hand went to her pocket. 'She seems really desperate.'

He laughed and said something that sounded pretty rude in Italian before he tacked on a polite translation in English. 'She is *really* devious.'

'She's probably suffering from postnatal depression—new mothers need *support*, you know.' As if he'd know the meaning of the word, she thought, throwing a look of seething contempt at him.

'She left her baby and you're *still* defending her. You really don't know your sister very well at all, do you?'

'I know enough, about her and about you too...'

His dark eyes narrowed on her flushed face his expression assessing as his long lashes rested briefly on the cutting angle of his cheekbones. 'Ah, so my reputation precedes me,' he drawled with a slow smile that Maya found almost as disturbing as his apparent ability to read her mind. 'So what has the absent mother been saying? Actually, don't bother, I can guess most of it, but maybe you should allow for a little bit of artistic licence on her part.'

'You probably make her feel inadequate!'

'Projection, much?'

The hot angry colour flew to her cheeks. 'You don't make me feel inadequate.' Her chin lifted to another defiant angle as she claimed boldly, 'Nobody makes me feel inadequate.'

The overreaction hinted at a vulnerability that was none of his business, he told himself, swiftly closing down that line of speculation.

'You don't strike me as an inadequate woman,' he mused, allowing his eyes to move in a slow sweep up her slim body before settling on her vivid heart-shaped face inside the frame of wild silky waves. The delicate features qualified as high on the catch-your-breath index but there was a determination to the round chin and a fierceness in her direct gaze that he seriously admired.

Taken aback by his response, Maya took an involuntary step away from him.

What do I strike you as, then? She pushed away the question as irrelevant and reclaimed the space she had given up. She tightened the sash on her robe another breath-restricting inch while somewhere in the back of her mind a voice reiterated, *It's past midday and you're still in your night clothes.*

'I wasn't talking about me.' Would he have been saying that if he'd seen the person she had been? Her defensive wall wavered and then held against the wave of self-disgust, and she met his dark stare with a semblance of calm.

He arched a dark brow. 'No?' His broad shoulders lifted in a shrug as his gaze moved beyond her to the closed bedroom door. 'If you say so…' He sighed and scrubbed a hand through his hair. 'I am here to see Mattio. Is he in here?' He tipped his head towards the right of the two doors they stood outside.

'That's my bedroom.' *God, Maya, how old are you?* she thought as she felt the heat rise up her neck. Deciding the best way to deal with the juvenile blush was to pretend it wasn't there, she glared up at him.

'You're not here to *see* him, you're here to take him away and I won't let you,' she asserted, sounding more confident than she felt at her ability to follow through with this claim.

'I haven't made any secret of what I'm here to do and if you're about to threaten me with the law again…' The prospect didn't alarm Samuele overly. 'I'd think that one through if I were you. Bring in the authorities on this one, and, red tape being what it is, I probably won't walk out of here with Mattio, but he *will* leave in the arms of some child protection social worker. And then when my court order granting me temporary guardianship comes through—which it will—I'll be able to take Mattio home.'

'You have a court order…?'

'I will have, soon.' It was not *strictly* a lie, but it would not have bothered Samuele if it had been.

'But,' she quavered out defiantly, 'Violetta is his mother! Don't courts *always* give a child to the mother?'

He gave a hard laugh and slung her a pitying look. 'That's often true—but it does kind of depend on the mother, don't you think?'

'Violetta's not here to defend herself,' Maya argued, knowing that words could be weaponised and a disparaging word here, a scathing comment there, could over time alter people's perception of someone, as she knew to her cost.

'Isn't that the point?' he suggested drily, looking bored with the discussion. 'She dumped a baby on a virtual stranger in a foreign country. That might raise a few legal brows.'

'Foreign…?'

'Mattio is Italian, he is an *Agosti*!'

'So is Violetta.'

'Not if Charlie has any say in the matter,' he shot back.

'Charlie?'

'Her next meal ticket,' he outlined with a thin smile.

'I'm not listening to you,' she bit back through clenched teeth.

'Because the truth hurts?'

'You twist everything I say.'

'Twist,' he echoed, raising his hands in a gesture that reinforced the scornful incredulity written on his face.

'For a woman to leave her baby...' Shaking her head, she scanned his face for any sign that he was capable of understanding what a massive thing that was. 'Have you *any* idea of what a terrible place she must have been in?'

'You really are determined to see her as some sort of victim, aren't you? I promise you that is the very last thing Violetta is. Look, Mattio is not your responsibility—'

'It's not about responsibility,' she retorted. 'It's about—' Struggling to put her feelings into words, she clenched her hands and tried to focus.

'It's about what?'

'It's about...' She made herself meet his eyes even though she knew the experience would not be comfortable. 'A child needs to be loved, to be wanted, and you don't really want him.'

'Now you're telling me what I want?'

'You just want to control everything.'

Samuele sketched a thin-lipped smile that he knew didn't reach his eyes. At that moment he'd settle for controlling his own baser urges, which at that moment... He shook his head slightly and thought, *Better not to go there*. The main thing was that he *was* in control.

'You really have swallowed Violetta's fiction hook, line and sinker, haven't you?'

'I haven't swallowed anything!' she fired back. 'I'm not some sort of gullible idiot—though I can see that it would suit you if I were!'

He didn't react immediately to her claim...there seemed little point. As he studied her face it was obviously she believed everything she was saying. His frustration levels threatened to bubble through his enforced calm.

He'd thought that he'd mentally prepared for every scenario he might face to get Mattio back, but in all of those he'd been dealing with Violetta, a known quantity.

This woman was definitely *not* a known quantity; in fact, she was the biggest unknown quantity that he had encountered—ever. A woman who looked as she did but made no conscious effort to use her allure was a mystery to him. She could bewitch a man with a flutter of her eyelashes if she wanted to, but all she did was try and batter him into submission with her totally flawed logic and stubborn arguments.

If he didn't have more important things on his mind, he might have been tempted to find out more about her, against his better judgement, though instinct told him that Maya Monk came with serious complications and possibly not the ones that he was armoured against. All the same, she was intriguing and quite incredibly beautiful.

How was it possible to want to taste a woman and at the same time want to...? He shook his head, despairing that anyone could be so wilfully stupid. This would have been a hell of a lot easier if she *hadn't* believed everything she was saying, and the fact he had not detected the sort of artifice he always expected from a beautiful woman made him uneasy.

His unease deepened when without warning a Eureka smile spread across her face.

'What about Violetta's mother? Could she come and look after Mattio until Violetta gets back?' Maya knew it was a compromise but maybe one that he might accept. 'What…why are you looking at me like that?'

'Your mother too, if I'm understanding your relationship correctly.'

'We're not in contact. Olivia has her own family.' Some of it was in her spare bedroom. 'And I have mine.' What would she not have given for her mum or sister to be in the same time zone right now?

If they had been, they would be here in this room offering her back-up and some much-needed baby advice.

'It's tough being rejected.'

She flinched, really disliking his ability to wander around inside her head. 'I'm not a victim. I was adopted as a baby, and, I told you, I have my own family now.'

'Olivia died six months ago.'

CHAPTER THREE

IT WAS LIKE watching the life story of a flower in time-lapse photography on a natural history programme; blooming, fading and shrivelling in mere seconds.

It was irrational, but he felt as guilty as hell for killing her hope.

'Sorry, I didn't know that.'

She was apologising to *him*? 'There's no need to be sorry, she was nothing to me.' From what Samuele had seen Olivia was a vain, selfish woman who had passed on all those delightful qualities to her daughter.

'Oh…no…me neither, I suppose… I mean, I didn't really know her either. How—?' she began and then stopped.

'She didn't suffer, did she?'

Samuele only knew the bare clinical facts, namely that Olivia had died after complications from a botched cosmetic surgery. He opened his mouth to share these when he met her anxious eyes and paused.

'No, she didn't,' he heard himself say.

Samuele caught a look of relief on her face before

she tipped her head in acknowledgement, and her expression was concealed by her wild mass of dark hair as she lowered her head.

So this was what lying to make someone feel better felt like—a novel experience but not one that he was likely to repeat any time soon.

'So this was something your *sister* clearly didn't share with you before she dumped her kid on you.'

Maya sighed. 'She was upset, and she probably assumed I already knew.' Even as she gave voice to the excuse Maya was thinking of the occasions that that there had been for her half-sister to tell her that their mother had died. 'She was desperate.' She felt ashamed of the doubt that she struggled to conceal but could hear in her own voice.

Not desperate, no—Samuele's eyes moved around the room—but the woman he knew would have to be very determined indeed to consider spending a night here.

'She is a widow with a baby, who is being undermined at every move.'

'You don't appear totally naive.' In his view, being idealistic was probably worse. 'So please listen to me when I tell you that this was totally planned, *cara*. She played you, as they say, for a sucker.'

'That's ridiculous!' *Was it?* Little details of the previous evening surfaced in her head that she would not even have thought about if it hadn't been for him planting seeds of doubt. 'I saw her, she was… Why would anyone…?' Her eyes suddenly widened. 'What did you call me?' Not Mia at least, said the catty voice in her head.

He shook his head in a pretty unconvincing attitude of bewildered innocence—she was pretty sure that Samuele Agosti was neither; it was hard to imagine he ever had been.

When she replayed it in her head the casual endearment on his lips sounded like honey, liquid and warm. Just thinking about it ignited another burst of heat low in her belly.

'She isn't coming back, you do know that?'

His expression came as near to sympathy as she'd seen, so she looked over his shoulder, refusing to allow the suspicions he had planted growing room in her head, worried because her hormones could be skewing her judgement. On the other hand, if what he said was true... Despite her determination the thought dropped into her consciousness and the ripples spread.

'I'm not leaving without Mattio,' Samuele stated.

I'm not leaving without Maya.

Maya swallowed past an emotional occlusion in her throat. She could suddenly see her dad so clearly, standing there smiling sunnily in response to being told that there was no parent accommodation available at the hospital—and besides, his little girl would be discharged from the overspill ward attached to the accident department after the cast that encased her broken arm had been checked by a doctor in the morning. She remembered willing him not to go and leave her in this big scary place and being glad he'd stayed even when she had cried that she wanted her mum, not him.

Mum had wanted to be there, he'd told her, but the rail strike meant she and Beatrice couldn't get back from the town where her sister had been competing in an athletics competition until the next day.

Her eyes lifted. There was no resemblance at all between the gangly dad of her memory, with his beard and untidy gingerish hair, and this tall, impossibly handsome man. But nevertheless, they had something in common.

'I need to see him,' he reiterated.

She offered up a suspicious look but couldn't bury the memories rising up in her...seeing the expression in her dad's eyes—the one that had made someone produce a chair for him to sit on.

After a moment she found herself nodding, not, she told herself, because of an expression in *anyone's* eyes, but because there was nothing she actually could do to prevent him.

She stood back and opened the door.

The curtains were drawn in the room; she had never reached the point of opening them. Light seeped between them and there was a lamp on the bedside table that cast more shadow than light.

Hovering uncertainly in the doorway, she watched him move across to the travel cot. He was not a man she would associate with hesitancy, but if he'd been anyone else that was how she would have termed his approach. As he reached it and looked down at the sleeping baby he was half turned to her so she could see his face in profile.

The subdued lighting exaggerated the dramatic bone structure of his face, and maybe it did the same to his expression, but what she saw or *thought* she saw was an almost haunted look of loss that made her feel almost as if she were intruding. Shaking her head at her irrational response as if to loosen the grip of the uncomfortable feelings, she quietly left the room without a word, wishing she could unsee that look. Empathy for him was the last thing she needed to be experiencing; she already felt bad enough for even imagining a fleeting similarity to her dad, who had been her hero. It felt like a betrayal.

She refused to concede that maybe Violetta's monster wasn't a *total* monster, so she focused on the indisputable fact that he quite definitely wasn't a hero, not her definition of one anyhow. She would save her empathy for the baby caught in the middle of a conflict.

Conscience pricking, she walked into her bedroom, musing over her struggle to feel anything sisterly towards baby Mattio's mother, despite her hot defence of the woman. She closed the door behind her, knowing that, as the walls were paper-thin between the two rooms, she'd hear a pin drop let alone someone making off with a baby.

Not that he would do that… On her way across the room she paused as she realised this confidence in him was actually based on nothing more than a very non-evidence-based gut feeling. Her self-reflective line of thought was abruptly terminated when she caught sight of herself in the mirror on the wardrobe door. *Just when she thought things could not get worse!*

She thought longingly of a shower as she left a trail of clothes in her wake, struggling to open a drawer in the tall heavy chest of drawers of stripped pine to reveal the neatly folded and brightly coloured selection of sweaters inside.

Walking out of the adjoining bedroom, Samuele was struggling to suppress immense waves of sadness, anger and guilt after looking at the child his brother had never met. Life is unfair; live it, he'd been told, except his brother hadn't lived and life wasn't just unfair—it was *bloody* unfair.

He hadn't been able to protect Cristiano, but he was sure as hell going to protect his child no matter what it took. Still lost in his thoughts, he turned his head in response to a sound at the exact moment he was in line with a crack in the slightly open door, delivering an image of a slim, graceful and totally naked figure sitting back on her heels as she pulled open a cavernous drawer.

Smooth, sleek, supple, with perfect curves, she looked like an iconic art deco figure made warm flesh.

He turned his head sharply away, a stab of self-disgust piercing his conscience as his body reacted independently of his brain to the indelible image printed on it.

Flinging the pair of jeans she had grabbed backwards onto the bed, Maya sifted through the sweaters and hastily selected one.

Still resisting the pull of the shower, she turned the basin taps on full and washed her face. She fought her way into her clothes and cast another despairing glance at her image in the mirror as, brush in hand, she decided to just give up on her hair, choosing instead to secure the wild mass of dark curls at the nape of her neck.

She was halfway through brushing her teeth when she heard a noise from the living-room monitor, followed by a gentle whimper from the adjoining bedroom.

'I think Mattio has woken up again!' Samuele called.

'I'll be right there!' she replied, hastily rinsing her mouth and remembering wryly not taking seriously Beatrice's claim during the early sleep-deprived days of motherhood that she'd struggled to get dressed before midday.

She erupted into the living room like someone reaching the finishing line of a sprint. 'What…why are you looking at me like that?'

He shook his head and crossed the room in a couple of fluid strides. Holding her gaze, he reached out and, before she could react, gently touched the corner of her mouth.

For a breathless moment their eyes clung as she tried desperately to hide the shuddering skin-tingling awareness that his touch had awoken.

If that was only a touch, imagine what a kiss would do to you, said the wicked voice in her head.

She already knew…the memory of the whisper of an almost-kiss surfaced from the place she had consigned it to and an uncontrollable shiver traced its way down her spine.

'Toothpaste,' he explained, sliding a tissue back into his pocket.

Her hand went to her mouth. Wearing clothes was meant to make her feel more confident and in control but they offered no protection whatsoever from his penetrating stare. 'Oh…right, thank you.' She shook herself and said briskly, 'I need to go and sort out Mattio.'

Samuele watched as she left the room. He could hear the gentle murmurs of her talking to the baby through the monitor and a moment later she returned carrying his nephew.

'Could you put that on the floor?' She nodded to the brightly coloured plastic mat beside the nappy stack. 'Yep, just unfold it for me, thanks.'

He continued to observe as she dropped to her knees and laid the baby on the padded plastic surface and jiggled with one of his feet before she unfastened the all-in-one affair he was wearing. The entire time she chatted unselfconsciously to Mattio, discussing what she was doing with the baby boy, who seemed to be listening to everything she was saying.

The change of nappy and clothes completed, she

settled back on her heels and gave a little grunt of satisfaction.

'You are really good at that,' he remarked thoughtfully. He knew he was not, and it was not exactly a short trip back to Italy.

'Beginners' luck,' she admitted. 'I do have a niece, although she is a few months older than Mattio. Beatrice, my sister, is already expecting another.'

'So were you both adopted?'

She shook her head as she got to her feet. 'No, Beatrice came along when I was one, a kind of miracle baby. Mum and Dad had been told they couldn't have children.'

'That must have put your nose out of joint.'

She smiled, clearly unoffended by the suggestion, which, he realised, had probably been made to her numerous times. 'No, our parents made absolutely sure we both knew we were special. Beatrice is my best friend.'

A muscle in his jaw clenched. 'Tell her that often,' he heard himself say.

Maya's liquid eyes held the beginning of understanding.

Although one of his rules in life was that he didn't explain himself, he inexplicably felt impelled to add abruptly, 'Because now I can't ever tell my brother that he was my best friend.'

'I should think he knew that, don't you? Sometimes you don't have to say anything.'

The gentle way she was looking at him, as though

he was no longer the enemy, unsettled him—or was it the fact that he liked the feeling that they might be coming to a better understanding of each other? No, that was far too dangerous. He didn't appreciate the way his thoughts were going. 'Could be. After all, he knew his wife cheated on him, but we never discussed that.' The closest they'd come was when they'd overheard a group of women in an adjoining restaurant booth discussing the latest rumour concerning Violetta, but Cristiano had cut him off before he could say a word. Subject closed—for ever.

I know you don't understand, but it's my life and I love her.

Her expression immediately froze over at his dig about Violetta. 'You just never give up, do you?'

'I have that reputation,' he responded coolly, accompanying his words with a lethal smile.

Lips tight, she glanced down at the baby, who was happily kicking his legs and blowing bubbles. 'Can you watch him while I go and get his feed?'

She didn't hang around long enough to see his nod of assent.

Samuele got to his feet. He could watch him but he could do very little else. Whenever he had tried to see Mattio, Violetta had always had a reason why it wasn't convenient. Perhaps he hadn't tried hard enough, which was why he was now little more than a stranger to his own nephew.

When Maya returned with the warmed bottle, Samuele was kneeling beside the baby, one large finger in

the tight baby grip of a pink chubby hand, but it was
the long thin red mark down the side of his face that
suddenly caught Maya's attention.

'He has sharp nails,' he mused, standing up and
looking slightly self-conscious.

'He isn't the only one,' she said, looking at the
scratch on his face and wondering if there were others on his back… The idea of him lost to passion like
that left a sour taste in her mouth.

'It's definitely not what you're thinking,' he said
drily as she settled with the baby in a chair.

She flashed him a startled look before bending her
head over the baby to hide the mortified heat that was
stinging her cheeks. 'You have no idea what I'm thinking,' she mumbled, focusing on the baby as he eagerly
attached his rosebud mouth to the teat and began to
enthusiastically suck.

Samuele knew *exactly* what she was thinking but
he didn't say anything until the bottle was empty and
she had carefully placed the baby over her shoulder
and was patting his back.

'This happened at the will reading.' He touched the
mark. 'The others have faded. It was Violetta's reaction to hearing that she would not have control of Cristiano's money, the money that, according to her, she
had *earned* as Cristiano's wife, and that apparently *I*
am stealing. Running away with Mattio is all part of
her vow to make me *regret it*.'

'That's a terrible, wicked thing to accuse someone
of!' she exclaimed, horrified. 'You really would say

anything to get what you want, wouldn't you? That's slander!'

'Only if it's not true, and there were witnesses there, including the lawyer.'

She shook her head, but Samuele could see, once again, the doubts about Violetta creeping into the edges of her previous certainty. Cuddling the baby in her arms, she got to her feet. 'There are two sides to every story.'

He sighed out his frustration as she settled Mattio in his little rocking chair. Maya eased her own chair protectively closer.

'I agree. There are always two sides, but it seems to me that you are only willing to hear one. Why are you so determined to believe that I am the one in the wrong? How do you think I knew you existed, knew your name, found this place?'

The groove between her feathery brows deepened as she shook her head.

'I had inside information from Charlie. Believe me or not, but the truth is that Violetta has a new, extremely wealthy boyfriend who very much wants to marry her.' Deluded fool.

'So you don't want another man bringing up your brother's baby?'

'The point is the other man doesn't want to bring up another man's baby or, for that matter, any baby at all.' He spelt out the situation with brutal brevity. 'Charlie wants Violetta but not Mattio. He has no interest in any child restricting his lifestyle.'

'So it was him who told you that Mattio was here?'

He nodded, seeing more cracks appear in her conviction and pushing home his advantage. 'He told me exactly where to find Mattio because it would suit him very well if I claimed the baby.' He held up a hand, the action drawing attention to the thin red line on his face and the tension round his sensual mouth. 'Yes, I know this might be another one of my very wicked lies, so how about you call her and hear the proof from the merry widow's own lips?'

'I can't call her because she left her phone here.'

'That was a nice touch. Let's face it, Maya, you are in no position to negotiate and there is a time limit on being awkward. Not that I'm suggesting you don't do it very well.'

Maya slung him an unamused smile, realising that if he did take the baby, it was going to be harder for his mother to reclaim him. Violetta needed to come back right now, and Maya was sure if she could just talk to her, her half-sister would understand.

'If you know who she's with and have his contact details, then let's call him, but let *me* speak to her. I'm sure by now she'll be feeling…' She petered out. She really wasn't qualified to guess how a woman who had walked away from her child felt. 'Guilty probably, so saying the wrong thing could tip her over the edge.'

'You think I can't be sensitive and tactful?' Maya pulled a face, which drew a reluctant laugh from him.

To hide the effect the unexpected sound had on her Maya channelled chilly disproval. It was a pity it only went skin-deep; to her shame, just under the surface she was all quivering, melting warmth. 'This isn't a joke.'

The smile in his eyes vanished, snuffing out like a candle. 'No, it isn't,' he said, producing a phone from his pocket. 'How about I put it on speaker? Then if I get too insensitive you can rescue the situation.'

He was being sarcastic, she could see that, but what she didn't understand was what he imagined he could achieve. Did he think he could bully Violetta into telling Maya to hand over her son? Even *imagining* such a situation brought her protective instincts to high-alert level and she'd only known the child existed for hours. Imagine if you'd carried and given birth…being apart from your baby would be like losing a part of yourself. Wouldn't it?

'You must see that the baby *needs* his mother.' She searched his face for any hint of understanding but, after a moment, sighed.

There was more give in a granite rock face.

'It depends on the mother. I don't know how well you knew Olivia, but you were far better off without her, I assure you. Just look how Violetta turned out.'

'We're not talking about me.' And they never would be because she would never invite this man into her head. 'I have no abandonment issues.'

She bit her lip. She was getting familiar with his expressive shrugs; he was able to convey a range of emotions with the slightest movement of his broad shoulders.

'What?' she snapped querulously, because he was staring at her in that unnerving way again.

'You have…' Samuele half lifted a hand and then shoved it safely back into a pocket. The last time he had touched her mouth— No, he wasn't going there again. 'Blood on your lip.'

A man who made a mistake could be forgiven, but if he knowingly repeated that mistake, he was a fool who didn't deserve forgiveness.

Samuele had never had any time for fools. Did it count as foolish, with the very recent memory of the heat that had stung through his body when he'd touched her mouth still fresh in his head, for his eyes to follow the tip of her tongue as it licked the pinprick drop of blood from the plump, pink outline of her bottom lip?

Probably not, but he hadn't followed through with the impulse to replace his finger with his mouth and continue the exploration. He knew his reasoning bore all the classic hallmarks of rationalisation, but there was such a thing as overthinking something.

He accepted that looking at her mouth, or any other part of Maya Monk, wasn't ever going to lead him down a path to inner peace. Luckily, he wasn't looking to take away inner peace from this encounter— just his nephew.

There was a tension in the room that Maya chose

to ignore as she nodded pointedly towards the phone he held.

After a moment he punched in a number and laid the phone on the coffee table between them. It was picked up almost immediately and a man replied, sounding distracted, possibly by the owner of the husky female laugh Maya could hear in the background.

'This is Samuele Agosti. Put Violetta on, will you, Charlie?'

There was a silence before the man on the other end began to babble. 'Samuele, it's great to hear your voice, but actually I can't help you—she's not with me...'

'Oh, for God's sake, give me that thing and get out.' There was the sound of rustling and banging and then what sounded like a door closing.

'He's gone. How did you know where I was?'

There was no betraying quiver in the voice; it was hard and cold and annoyed, but Maya knew without doubt that she was listening to her half-sister.

'Well, you're not with your child so where else would you be?'

'You found him! Damn, that was quick,' she snapped petulantly. 'Clever old you. I really wanted you to sweat.'

The most shocking thing for Maya was that Samuele didn't look even slightly surprised by this vicious, vindictive statement. Instead, he looked...she searched the angles and hollows of his face and the word *dangerous* floated into her head. The ruthless, relentless quality she had been aware of in him was in sharp focus as he allowed the moment to stretch before responding.

'You succeeded.' His glance shifted across to where Maya stood like a frozen statue, her hand pressed to her mouth, horror shining in her eyes.

Breaking eye contact, he shifted his weight from one foot to the other to move her into the periphery of his vision, ignoring the weight of uneasy guilt in his chest.

He had no time to be gentle; she *needed* to hear this. The truth was brutal—everyone learnt that lesson sooner or later. Yes, sometimes having your eyes opened hurt, but walking around with them tightly shut was dangerous, and a woman who'd reached her age should have stopped believing that every person was good and honest.

'I was hoping you'd have to suffer for much longer than this.' The petulance was now laced with viciousness. Maya felt almost numb now as she heard her half-sister hiss, 'Because you deserve it after you turned my own husband against me and stole what's mine. I deserve that money!'

'Would that I could have turned him against you, but he was loyal to you to the end.'

The bone-deep weariness and despair in Samuele's voice finally penetrated Maya's own personal misery. It had all been an act and she had fallen for it.

'You wanted to see me suffer, I get that, but isn't this all a little bizarrely complicated, even for you?'

'If I'd tried to vanish in Italy your contacts would

have found me in thirty seconds and I needed to be in London to get my hair done—my colourist here is simply the best.' Her laugh that made Maya think of glass breaking rang out before Violetta added, 'And anyhow London definitely solved the babysitting problem. It was a toss-up, I thought, between that and having someone burn down your bloody castle, but this was more of a "two birds with one stone" thing. I told you that you'd regret cutting me out of the money. Next time I'll get even more inventive, so don't relax just yet, will you, darling?'

'Cristiano left you very well provided for.' Samuele struggled to keep his voice free of the disgust churning in his belly. 'You don't need Mattio's half of the Agosti estate as well.'

'Your brother always did what you told him, but at least your investment advice paid off. I do have a very nice sum, you're right, but half the estate is worth a fortune.'

'It's Mattio's.'

'And Mattio is mine, but maybe now that you've found him I might let you keep him.'

'How much do you want?'

'Oh, darling, you can be so crude. You may hold the purse strings but I hold the baby, so play nice or I might change my mind.'

'I'm listening.'

'So you've met Mother's little mistake, have you? Mummy said she wouldn't be a problem or try and encroach in our lives, but it never occurred to me that she'd actually be useful.'

Samuele was glad that Maya had moved out of his line of vision; he didn't want to see her reaction to that disgusting remark. 'Get to the point,' he bit out.

'I see my future with Charlie.'

'And his millions,' he added contemptuously.

'Well, I wouldn't marry a poor man, would I?' she cooed.

He didn't bother replying.

'It suits me for you to have Mattio right now. Charlie is not really into babies, but there's always the possibility that I might just change his mind about that.' And with that, she hung up.

After any conversation with Violetta, Samuele usually felt as though he needed a shower and this was no exception. He didn't know at what point Maya had left the room or how much she had heard.

She was standing in the kitchen, her head bent. She had dragged her hair across one shoulder and was anchoring it there with her forearm, revealing the sculpted hollows of her collarbones, the delicately defined angle of her jaw and the elegant length of her neck.

She didn't immediately turn when he entered but the added level of quivering tension in her body made it clear she knew he was there.

'I don't know how much of that you heard…?'

Maya's arm fell away and her hair tumbled free as she spun around to face him.

'Enough to know you were right, I was wrong, she was using me and now you've got what you want.' She struggled to keep her voice flat, and struggled harder to push away the overwhelming self-pity, ashamed she was making this personal because the only person who should be considered in this scenario was the baby in the next room. 'I suppose you want me to pack up his things?' Without any warning her dignity was drowned in a rush of blinding anger.

'Is it all about the challenge for you? The winning? I suppose you'll lose interest in him now you've won,' she threw out, not even sure she believed it but wanting to hurt him because—well, she was not about to give him the benefit of the doubt.

Or maybe she just didn't want to be the only one hurting here.

Samuele tensed, every muscle in his face clenching as his face blanked, and anger bit deep at the insult. She had unerringly targeted his pride, questioning his integrity and implying he had no conscience.

He knew many men who were successful because they possessed little or no conscience. When it came to making money a conscience was something of a hindrance so he hid his, which made it doubly ironic that he was insulted now because he'd succeeded.

But when their gazes connected there was no spite in hers, just a mixture of sadness and pain, a pain so deep it took a real effort for him to detach himself from the emotions he saw there. His own anger deflated, leaving a vague sense of utterly irrational guilt in its place.

'This child doesn't have a father, which is not my definition of winning.' He arched a brow. 'What's yours?'

Maya's brow puckered, the muscles on her face quivering as her eyes softened and went liquid. 'I'm so sorry, your brother must have been very young when he died.'

He watched her fighting back tears and struggled to imagine just how uncomfortable that degree of empathy must be to live with as he found himself revealing, 'He tried to hang on to see his son, but he didn't make it. He was the bravest man I have ever known.'

Samuele had never discussed his brother or the battle he had fought with anyone, so why was he suddenly opening up to Maya, of all people? He dodged the answer and swore under his breath. 'You don't have anything to be sorry for.'

'When I lost my dad I bottled up my feelings, but when I actually talked about them—'

In a voice that could have wilted green shoots on a plant, he cut across her. It was for her own sake really; if she started wandering around in his head, she would definitely find more than a few things that she didn't like. 'I appreciate the sharing,' he drawled sardonically, 'but—'

This time it was Maya who shut him down. 'I get the message.'

She did. If he was one of those people who thought

admitting to emotions was a sign of weakness, that was his business; it was the baby her heart ached for. Being taught by example that to *suck it up* was what real men did… God, it was so depressing.

As she thought of the baby her eyes softened. She might have been abandoned but there was never a moment in her life after she was adopted that she had doubted she was loved. It was those early years that had made her tough enough to survive Edward's concerted campaign of destruction.

'What will you ever tell him about his mother?' *Oh, God, I said that out loud!*

Bracing herself for another one of his icy put-downs, she maintained a defiant stance as she slowly turned to face him.

'I would write her out of his life if that was possible.'

No ice, just a cool statement of fact, and while she sympathised with his attitude, she still didn't think it was the right one. But then it wasn't her business, was it? she reminded herself.

'Isn't it possible? Isn't she giving you custody of Mattio?' Giving him away as if he were simply a piece of excess baggage. That was when she'd had to leave the room; if she'd stayed there another moment her feelings would have got the better of her and she'd have started yelling down the phone at her half-sister.

'Nothing is ever that simple with Violetta. It suits her now to have me take Mattio back to Italy, but she won't relinquish her maternal control willingly,' he predicted. 'And once she's got Charlie to the altar…

Let's just say she can be very persuasive indeed,' he finished grimly, no doubt thinking of the custody battle that lay ahead.

'Oh…I'm sorry.'

He arched a sardonic brow.

'Well, you'd be better for Mattio than she would be. Actually, anyone would,' Maya said honestly.

'Wow, faint praise indeed,' he drawled, the smile in his voice warming his eyes and making her want to smile back.

She fought the urge and dived for the door. 'I'll start packing his things up.'

CHAPTER FOUR

MATTIO HAD DOZED off in his little chair. Coming into the living room behind her, Samuele watched as Maya tenderly tucked a light blanket around him and began to pick up the baby items strewn around.

Feeling a stab of self-disgust that even in a time like this he could appreciate, actually more than appreciate, the tightness of her behind under the snugly fitting denim, he cleared his throat.

'I have been thinking.'

One hand on her thigh, the other outstretched to scoop up a soft toy that had found its way under a side table, she lifted her head and looked up at him from under the frame of curling lashes. She was oblivious to the fact the action made her square-necked cobalt-blue sweater gape, giving him a tantalising glimpse of her lacy bra and the suggestive creamy swell of her smooth cleavage. The shadow of her nipples under the lace might have been his imagination which was, to his own annoyance, clearly working overtime.

'Come with us.' The offer was made not because

of his recent testosterone rush but *despite* it—it was a purely practical suggestion, he told himself, devoid of any personal feelings.

Purely practical would have been putting an ocean or three between this woman and you, pointed out the voice in his head.

He ignored it and the insulting implication he was not totally in control. For someone who had been born with a hot temper and a tendency to act before his brain was in gear, he was conscious of the need to maintain control at all times. Allowing their emotions and appetites full rein had been the downfall of both his father and brother, so Samuele's life was ruled by his determination to ruthlessly suppress any similar tendencies when and if they ever surfaced in himself.

Maya dropped the toy and came upright with a jerk that made her hair bounce angrily before settling in a silky tumble down her back. 'Is that some sort of joke?'

'No, it's… Have you been crying?' he asked, observing the dampness on her cheeks with a tightening in his chest.

Maya was always alert and very defensive about anyone assuming that, just because she looked delicate, she *was* delicate. There was something patronising in people thinking she needed to be given special treatment.

So she had zero qualms about lying.

'No, I have not.'

It was crazy! This time yesterday she had not even known this baby boy existed. Maybe it was the fact they had both been abandoned that had brought out these painfully intense protective feelings in her?

'Well, you look—'

'I have *not* been crying—though God knows the way this day is going, it would be small wonder if I had!'

He lifted his hands in an open-palmed pacific gesture. 'Fine, you have not been crying.' He shrugged. 'I have a flight home arranged.'

She had been prepared to hear him out in stony silence, but her curiosity won that battle. 'Where is home?' Where would she imagine Samuele living? She wouldn't be imagining him at all, she reminded herself, but who knew if his voice might continue to seep into her dreams…?

She gave a little shiver. On any measurement scale their first chance encounter had not exactly been a cosmic event and yet it had lingered in her mind. More than lingered, if she was honest, thinking of that voice in her dreams, the touch she woke up remembering, which was an invention of her subconscious, because he had never touched her. Did that merest whisper of a kiss even count?

Now fate, or whatever you liked to call it, had thrown them together once more. Not just a nudge this time, but a full-on red-light collision, and they were connected for ever by Mattio.

He still hadn't touched her.

'Tuscany, outside Florence. The estate has been in our family for generations.' And very briefly large sections temporarily not. The realisation that his father had been selling off piecemeal vast tracts of the estate and splitting up the world-renowned Agosti art collection, just to keep his second wife, Samuele's stepmother, in private jets, luxury yachts and jewels to wear when she lost yet another fortune at the gaming tables, had caused Samuele to abandon his medical degree course midway through.

Medicine might provide status, respect and job satisfaction, but if he wanted to succeed in his determination to restore his family's heritage he needed money, the sort of money that the financial services sector could provide for someone who was successful. And Samuele was hugely successful, his rise had been meteoric and he had never regretted his decision, not once.

Before his father's death he had discreetly, through a series of anonymous holding companies, managed to reacquire seventy per cent of the estate that his father had sold. After his death there had been no need for discretion and the restoration of the Agosti villa in Florence had been completed the previous year.

He had expected success to feel more...*victorious*? He pushed the thought away. The truth was, it was hard to be enthused about anything since Cristiano's death. And now he had someone to hand the reclaimed heritage on to. He had Mattio.

He would always put Mattio's needs ahead of every other consideration, including his own conscience.

'I have a private plane waiting.' He said it in the casual way that, in Maya's experience, only people with a lot of money spoke about such things. 'I'll need a nanny for Mattio.'

'I'm not a nanny!'

'*Dio*, I wasn't offering you the job.'

He was secure in his self-control, but inviting this woman to live under the same roof as him on any sort of permanent basis, given the chemistry that existed between them, would break too many of his self-imposed boundaries when it came to allowing women into his life. And if ever he'd met a woman who was incapable of recognising a boundary, let alone staying the right side of one, Maya Monk was it.

He didn't need a woman like her in his life—actually he didn't need any woman. Of course, there were women he had sex with occasionally—he needed sex, the same as any man—but they never threatened his inner peace.

Another word for loneliness, mocked his inner voice, but he didn't care if it was true. Isolation was preferable to the option both his father and brother had embraced: marrying wives who'd taken them for every penny and made them smile while they did it.

Embarrassed heat stung Maya's cheeks. There was nothing like refusing a job you hadn't been offered to make a girl feel stupid. 'Oh, well…my mistake.' Her firm little chin lifted, defiance exuding from every pore as she added mutinously, 'But it sounded to me like you were.'

His gaze drifted from her narrowed eyes to her sensuous mouth that couldn't look thin and mean, even though she was clearly trying. When it came to a live-in nanny, he would definitely not choose one that looked like Maya Monk. A world where she was a permanent feature in his life without her sharing his bed was an absolute non-starter... No, the person he had in mind was sturdy and no-nonsense, radiating a comforting, calm, kind vibe. Would it be sexist to put any of those things in the ad?

'I travel light, and I have no experience of babies,' he admitted, thinking he had even less experience of women who made him laugh. 'Let alone travelling with one.' Logic told him there had to be more to that endeavour than there appeared. 'And it's going to take me a little time to find a suitable nanny. In the interim, I was thinking that you could...help out with Mattio. I've watched you with him—you're good with him, he knows you and you seem like a...safe pair of hands.' With a soft heart, which of course was what he was counting on.

'So you don't want a nanny, you just want an unqualified, unpaid dogsbody!'

'Are there qualifications for doing someone a favour?' he asked with a shrug. 'And payment isn't an issue—name your price.'

She reacted huffily to the suggestion that she could be bought. 'I can't be bought.'

He fought the impulse to share his cynical view that that fact alone made her unusual, if not unique.

'Not a very practical response, but fine, if that's what you want, I won't pay you.'

She threw him a narrow-eyed look of dislike. 'I suppose you assume that just because I'm female I know about babies.'

Female... Yes, she was... The provocative blood-heating image of her slim, smooth, naked body, *very* female naked body, floated into his head, making it hard to stick to his point. 'You really could do with some lessons in selling yourself.'

'I'm not trying to sell myself,' she said, her voice barely audible beyond the sound of her low shallow breaths, which made the subsequent decibel rise all the more apparent as she suddenly added, 'And I really don't care what *you* or anyone else thinks about me. I care what *I* think about me.' To his ears it had all the hallmarks of a classic *she protests way too much* denial.

She was too busy trying to inject some much-needed neutrality into her voice to notice the thoughtful expression that slid across his face. 'And I've already said no.'

'Yes, you did.'

You didn't have to do much reading between the lines to work out that once she *had* cared about what someone thought, and that someone had done some serious damage to her self-confidence.

She had recovered because she was obviously a strong woman, but there were always scars...even if they weren't visible. He'd come across men like that; ones who made themselves feel big to disguise the fact they were hollow and weak. He would have liked to get his hands on—

He forced himself to de-escalate his growing antagonism towards this faceless creation of his imagination, the man who'd probably tapped into the passion he sensed in Maya, who had maybe made it harder for her to enjoy it with the next man who came along.

But he was not that man.

'You wouldn't be doing it for me,' he emphasised. 'You'd be doing it for Mattio. What's a few weeks out of your life? The poor kid hasn't had much continuity in his so far.'

Even a compulsive liar had to speak the truth occasionally, Maya thought sardonically as her half-sister's words floated through her head. *You don't know what Samuele is capable of.*

Well, she now knew one thing he was capable of after this breathtakingly blatant attempt to play on her feelings for Mattio.

'For future reference,' she told him crisply, 'I don't respond well to moral blackmail. Not that there will be—a future, I mean,' she tacked on, wincing, because the only thing she'd managed to do was make it sound as though they had a past.

They didn't have a past, present or future. She had spent more time in the company of the woman at the checkout till at her local supermarket than this man, and she actually knew more about her!

It was just the entire off-the-scale hothouse weirdness of everything about the last few hours that had fed this strange feeling of intimacy between them, utterly misplaced intimacy, she told herself.

'Sorry, that was below the belt.'

She suddenly caught an expression in his face and wondered if he felt guilty. If he did, it couldn't be *that* guilty. It wasn't in his nature to give up, and when one tactic failed you tried an alternative one. He didn't disappoint her.

'I need your help and if you can put aside your dislike of me… I mean, you don't have to like me or trust me, and any practical inconvenience I will sort out with your employer or whatever. Will you promise to think about it?'

She struggled not to feel disarmed by his sincerity, but knew she was losing the battle as she felt her antagonism melting away. 'How long before you need to know?'

He glanced at the thin metal banded watch on his wrist. 'Five…no, make that four minutes.' He looked at her, one dark brow arched, and produced a white grin that would have given the devil a run for his money—a very attractive devil.

She gave a small laugh of disbelief.

'And I would really appreciate your input into the recruitment of the nanny too,' he said, dangling the suggestion like a carrot of temptation.

She breathed out heavily. 'I just can't…' Her voice trailed away as the exhaustion she'd been holding at bay with sheer willpower suddenly hit her, like walking into a wall, and bone-deep weariness came flooding in.

'Are you all right?' He stood braced, looking as though he was fully prepared to catch her if she fell, which was a good thing because she really felt as if she might go down.

She pulled herself to her full height, but she still had to tip her head back a long way to look him in the face.

'I'm fine,' she grouched irritably, wishing she could throw something more than his concern back in his face, then sighed as she felt impelled to add, 'Thank you.'

'You need to sit down. You're having a vasovagal attack.'

'A what?'

'You're going to faint.' Taking matters into his own hands, he took her by the shoulders and manoeuvred her onto the nearest sofa. One finger pressed into the middle of her chest sent her backwards while he lifted her legs onto the cushions.

'I don't faint.' In her head it was a firm, calm statement, but sadly it emerged as a weak little whisper. Maybe she would just lie there until the world stopped spinning. Things were a bit vague and hazy, and she couldn't even work up the enthusiasm to react when she felt cool fingers taking the pulse on her wrist. 'Who made you the expert on fainting anyhow?'

Eyes closed, she missed the look that crossed his face.

'I suppose you've been making girls swoon all your

life,' she observed waspishly as she experimentally opened her eyes to discover the world had stopped spinning.

'Take it slowly,' he cautioned as she lifted herself up onto an elbow.

A massive surprise when she ignored him and sat up, swinging her legs to the floor. 'Did you get much sleep last night?'

It seemed like a century ago since she had opened her door to her half-sister, and the memories were already meshed into a kaleidoscope of intertwined images.

It had been one hit on top of another. The exhaustion she was feeling was not just about sleep deprivation; it was emotional.

'Take this.' She curled her fingers around the warm teacup. 'You can sleep on the plane.'

She flung him a look and grimaced as, cradling the cup between her two hands, she lifted it to her lips and drank. 'I don't take sugar.' She took another sip anyway. 'I can't just drop everything...my job...' Her voice trailed away. She was expecting her redundancy notice to arrive any day now, not that that made any difference.

'Where do you work?'

She named the department store. 'I'm a window dresser.'

'But I saw the sketches...'

Her glance went to the folders stacked behind the folded architect's table, which she'd intended to put away in the spare room. 'My sister and I had plans to start a small fashion label, but she got back together with her husband, and start-up businesses need some serious capital and time investing in them... In the meantime, I do actually like my job.'

'Don't married women work?'

'It would be a long commute. Beatrice lives in San Macizo.'

His mobile black brows lifted. 'Yes, I can see that would be pushing it...' He paused, a frown corrugating his brow. '*Beatrice?* As in the—'

She cut him off. 'Yeah, I have royal connections.'

'Who could surely give you the capital you need to start up your business?'

At the hint of criticism in his voice she fired back angrily, 'They have offered and I refused.'

'Interesting.' She didn't ask what was so interesting and he didn't elaborate. 'So you have a niece, and now you have a nephew too.' He watched closely as the shock of recognition flickered in her eyes.

'Yes.'

'I imagine that you'd do anything for your niece?'

'Obviously,' she responded, indignant that there could be any doubt about that before she saw the point he was making.

It was true she would do anything for little Sabina, who had an adoring mother and father, who would never ever be abandoned or made to feel she was not worthy of love. She looked up at Samuele over the rim of her teacup, feeling lighter as she shrugged off the invisible but very real weight of indecision.

Why would she do any less for her nephew, who was so much worse off than her niece?

'I'll do it.'

It would be fine, she told herself. All she had to do was remember that she could not fall too deeply in love with her nephew because, in reality, parting was inevitable.

The uncle…well, there was no danger of love being involved there, but she would have to keep some sort of check on the surges of attraction that might put her in danger of doing something stupid.

Like flying off to Italy with a man you barely know where your lack of childcare skills is going to be outed very quickly.

CHAPTER FIVE

SHE STRUGGLED TO shake the feeling that she was there under false pretences as Samuele's staff deferred to her on every matter to do with the baby on board.

Apart from an interval when he became fretful, which, according to one sympathetic steward who seemed knowledgeable about such things, meant that he was probably teething, he'd been no trouble at all.

'Look at those hot little cheeks, bless him. We didn't sleep for a week when our eldest was teething,' she said, setting out the bottle of formula Maya had not needed to request, but had magically appeared.

As Maya jogged up and down later, Mattio in her arms, she could appreciate how much harder this might have been if there were more than the one other passenger on board. Samuele was certainly not going to complain about the noise of a grizzling baby, but even he had spent most of the flight locked in a private cabin where she presumed he was working, only appearing when they were about to land to ask, in what she felt was a critical way, if she'd had any sleep.

Did she look that bad?

'He's teething,' she said stiffly, nodding to the baby, who had just nodded off himself.

'Oh.'

Maya quite enjoyed seeing him look out of his depth. She could imagine that it was probably a once-in-a-decade thing, so she didn't let on that she was too.

Once they disembarked a well-oiled machine seemed to spring into action, making the transfer into a luxury four-wheel-drive painless and swift.

The only blip in this process was when the passenger door was opened by one of the team whose sole purpose in life appeared to be saying *'sì'* to Samuele. Though to be fair his attitude did not suggest he required deference. He was relaxed with all his staff, who seemed pretty at ease with him too. Maya, whose nervous system was on permanent red-alert mode around him, felt quite envious. She hesitated at the car door. She had intended to sit next to the baby in the back seat, though perhaps there was no such safe distance when it came to Samuele.

'Is there a problem?' Samuele sounded impatient. She noticed he had got changed on the flight and the black jeans that greedily clung to his muscular thighs seemed a very valid reason not to sit beside him. God knew when he'd found the time to swap clothes, but then it seemed to Maya that he did everything at a million miles an hour. He was not, she decided, the sort of person to take time out to appreciate a sunset or a view. Did he ever actually relax?

'I was wondering if we'd see much of Florence. I've never been there but I understand it's very beautiful.'

'Another day I'll give you a guided tour.'

'Oh, I didn't mean—'

'Get in, Maya.'

She got in rather than make a fuss and any concerns she had about making stilted conversation were unnecessary because they were barely outside the city limits when she fell asleep.

When she woke, confused, her head propped against the padded headrest, a blanket from the back seat thrown over her, she was too muzzy-headed to think about how it had got there. Samuele wasn't in the car.

She rubbed her eyes, knowing that it was a given that her hair would look as though there were small animals living somewhere in the wild mass of curls. She took in her surroundings. The car was stationary and they were parked at the side of a narrow empty road where the trees lining the road ahead and behind had thinned to reveal what was the most incredible panoramic view she had ever seen in her life. She'd clearly been wrong: Samuele did stop to look at the view.

She gave the peacefully dozing baby in the back seat a quick glance before she unfastened her belt and exited the car. Her nostrils flaring at the pungent scent of pine and the wild thyme that released its sweet scent into the air, she picked a path across to where Samuele stood, his tall figure dark against the backdrop of a deep cerulean-blue sky.

'Sorry I fell asleep...oh, my, it's so beautiful.' She

sighed, her eyes drawn to the view that stretched out before them. Against the distant backdrop of the purple hills the undulating fields were a patchwork of colours, gold with wheat and green grazed by animals impossible to identify at this distance. The separate areas were defined by rows of statuesque pine and dotted with sculptural cypresses, and ribbons of water gleamed as they wound their way down the sloping hills that, to her uneducated eyes, seemed to be covered with the regimented neatness of vineyards.

For a long time she said nothing. 'It's almost… *spiritual.*' The words emerged without any conscious thought and a moment later she gave an embarrassed little laugh and angled a look up at him. Samuele was no longer staring at the landscape, but looking at her, the expression on his face making her insides quiver.

'That probably sounds stupid.'

'Not at all. It's taken some people a lifetime to see that, and some,' he added heavily, 'never do.'

He redirected his stare to the vista but there was a brooding quality to his stare now that hadn't been there before.

'When do we reach…your home?'

'We have.' He opened his hands wide to encompass the land that stretched out before them. 'We have actually been on the estate for the past twenty minutes, and the village is about five minutes back there. You'll be able to see the house once we come out on the other side of that copse.'

'I had no idea that it was so…vast,' she admitted,

making some serious adjustments to her preconceptions of the Agosti heritage. 'You own an entire village?'

'My family has cared for this land for years and it has cared for us…and many others in return. Until recently.'

'Recently?' she probed warily, wondering if he was alluding to his brother's death.

'My father stripped everything of value he could and sold off the rest to keep his wife in private jets and fuel her main hobby which was—and presumably still is—gambling,' Samuele said heavily. 'She went into rehab after my father's death, where she met her new husband; in a twist of irony, he owns a string of hotel casinos.'

'When you said his wife, was she not your mother?'

'My mother is dead. My father's second wife was Cristiano's mother. I remember that she adored him as a baby but as soon as he passed the cute baby stage she treated him pretty much like an out-of-date handbag.'

The calming effect of the beauty of the land he loved so much, the land that would never hurt him, evaporated as he dwelt on the destructive emotion his father had called love. Even at the end, when he'd known that the woman he'd worshipped was having affair after affair, he'd still defended her to his eldest son. And then, to Samuele's despair, exactly the same fate had befallen Cristiano.

'She didn't consider she had an addiction problem so my father didn't either. His duty to the land, his tenants, his family…he sacrificed them all for this in-sanity of selfishness, which went disguised as love.'

The delivery was flat and even but despite, or maybe because of, his measured neutrality Maya could feel the emotions throbbing in every syllable.

'But the land—you said this is yours now…?'

'I started buying it back anonymously as soon as I could afford to, and now it is almost back to what it once was.' He still had hopes of tracking down the last few elusive classical sculptures that would complete the art collection that had rivalled many museums.

'Wow, that couldn't have been cheap…' She flushed as his eyes swivelled her way. 'Sorry, I didn't mean to sound nosy.'

'Yes, it wasn't…er…*cheap, cara*.'

To her relief he seemed amused, not offended.

'I am an investment banker, so raising capital is what I specialise in, and the finance industry pays ex-tremely well.' He had not drifted into finance, he had deliberately plotted a course, and the rewards, not the job satisfaction, had been his motivation for doing so.

He inhaled, drawing in the sweet clean air as he scanned the horizon. To Maya, it seemed as though he was letting the peace, the sense of continuity over the ages, visibly seep into him.

'So the estate is a hobby?'

He continued to look into the distance. 'No, finance is my hobby. The estate is my life.' He turned to face her. 'So, are you ready?'

Caught staring at him, she shifted guiltily and began

to move towards the four-wheel-drive. 'I'm sorry I fell asleep…' she said again, skipping to fall into step beside him.

It was a subject he did not particularly want to think about. He closed it down with a light teasing reply. 'Relax, you don't drool.' But he couldn't close down the images that stubbornly remained inside his head or the memory of the scent of her hair as it tickled his neck.

After the second time of nudging her head back onto the headrest, he had finally let it stay where it kept falling against his shoulder.

'Sorry, I wasn't much company.'

'A woman who doesn't talk while I'm driving is my kind of perfect.'

Maya huffed a little as she tried to keep pace with his long-legged stride. 'Did you take classes in sexist chauvinism?'

He flashed her a look, all white teeth and testosterone.

'No, I am totally self-taught.'

The exchange had brought them level with the luxury off-roader that stood in the sculpted shade of a cypress tree. 'Your mother must be so proud of you,' she muttered, raising herself on tiptoe to look through the back window she had cracked open before she'd left the car. Mattio had not moved an inch.

'She's dead, remember.'

She shot him a contrite look. 'That was a stupid thing for me to say!'

'Oh, I don't know, it was quite funny. Relax,' he

said matter-of-factly, opening the passenger door for her. 'I barely remember her.' Sometimes a memory would surface, triggered by a scent or a familiar object. 'And my life did not lack female influence for long,' he added in a tone hard enough to cut through diamond. 'She was barely cold in her grave before I had a step-mother and, four months later, a half-brother.'

Her eyes, widened in comprehension, flew to his face. 'Four months?'

His fingers curved around her elbow to give her a steadying boost into the seat of the high-level vehicle, which brought her face level with his.

'A married man having an affair...' he mocked. 'Who'd have thought?' Not Maya, clearly, and her na-ivety made him perversely want to shock her more. 'When I was going through my father's papers I found some of my mother's things.' Untouched and gather-ing metaphorical dust, since they'd been consigned to a filing cabinet with the other *unimportant* items.

'There were some legal documents dated the day before her death. It turns out he had served her with divorce papers, something that was not revealed in the inquest, I would imagine, seeing as I think they might have had a bearing on their verdict of accidental overdose. Maybe if there had been a suicide note...?'

The way he relayed the details, with a total absence of any emotion, was somehow almost *more* shocking than the story itself.

It made her wonder just how deep he'd buried the trauma. She never doubted there *was* trauma because

Maya knew from experience that it never, ever went away, not until you faced it.

'I suppose there are some things you can never know.' Given the story, his attitude to marriage and women was hardly surprising.

He met her sympathetic gaze with a look that was dark, hard and unforgiving. 'Oh, I know, I know full well that my mother killed herself because she was being traded in, because she didn't give a damn about what or who she left behind—namely me.'

He'd thought the words plenty of times, but he'd never actually said them out loud before. The pity he could see shining in her luminous eyes was the reason why.

Samuele looked away from those eyes, asking himself yet again what it was about Maya Monk that made him open himself up this way. He had revealed more about himself in the space of the last few hours than he had told anyone—ever.

'I don't need your pity.'

'Good, because you haven't got it. There's a difference between pity and compassion, you know! You're angry with a parent for leaving you—believe you me, that doesn't make you unique around here, Samuele. Your mother found it impossible to carry on living but that doesn't mean she stopped loving you.'

He climbed into the vehicle after her, staring stonily ahead as he reversed out of the clearing at speed.

'Sorry,' he said as they hit a particularly bad pothole that almost jolted Maya out of her seat. 'Resurfacing this road is due to start next month. If we were approaching from the other way, the road is almost civilised.' He was watching her as he turned the corner; he liked to see people's reactions as they got their first glimpse of the castello.

Maya's jaw dropped as she took in the square towers in each corner of the massive sandstone edifice and the teethlike projections high up along the walls between them. It seemed to ramble, if you could use such a word for such a formidable-looking building. 'You live in a palace!'

'Castello di Agosti is classified as a castle. My family have lived here since the thirteenth century, apart from a short period when it was used as a hospital during the Second World War.'

'It's…'

'I have never seen a ghost.'

'I wasn't going to ask that.' But, of course, now she was thinking it. 'Are there many suits of armour?'

'A few, hopefully not dusty. Relax, the place has been totally renovated with all mod cons. You look more apprehensive than the tenants did when I introduced some new eco-farming methods. We have a long-term strategy here.'

They were driving along a wide, smoothly surfaced driveway now that wound its way through lush parkland. As the road divided she saw a field with horses in.

'Years ago our stud was world-renowned. We've just started building up a breeding programme again in a small way.'

It seemed to Maya that nothing here was built on a small scale.

'Oh, my!' She twisted her head to see the gardens that they were passing, stone terrace after stone terrace spilling flowers above a formal walled garden with a series of classical looking fountains.

She settled back into her seat as they drove away from the castle and through an archway into a gravelled area surrounded by low stone buildings.

The car stopped and a small welcoming party appeared: two young men in white shirts and dark trousers, who began to unload their luggage; a woman with no visible waist and a lovely smile and another young man, who were introduced by Samuele as the housekeeper, Gabriella, and his private secretary.

While the housekeeper got tearful over Mattio, Maya watched Samuele and his secretary talking quietly. A few moments later she could almost see him shrugging off his city persona; here he was king of the castle, though a very chilled-out king. In fact, he looked more relaxed than she had imagined possible.

'I have some things to attend to, so I will see you at dinner. Gabriella will look after you,' Samuele said, turning to her.

'I don't expect you to look after me,' she blurted.

He tipped his head. 'You are our guest.' There was nothing in his words, but the light in his eyes made her stomach muscles quiver.

'*Our*...is there a...do you have a...? Are you married or anything?' She paused awkwardly, the idea he wasn't single sending panic that was quite out of proportion with the possibility through her body as she stood there kicking herself for not asking earlier.

'Not even *anything* at this present moment. It was just a figure of speech.'

At the outset Maya had no idea what her role was classified as being while she was here, and she had half expected to be accommodated in the servants' quarters. Although if what she had seen was any indication the servants' quarters would be pretty five star.

There were several gasp-out-loud moments as she was led by the housekeeper, who'd offered to carry the travel seat that Mattio was snuggled in, an offer Maya declined, through the vaulted hallway with its stone walls and up a grand staircase that divided into a gallery at the top.

'The frescoes are in the west wing,' Gabriella explained as she led the way along a long corridor that could have easily accommodated a couple of football pitches.

Maya nodded, as though she knew about wings or frescoes.

When they finally reached the suite of rooms she had been allocated it was clear that she was not expected to slum it. She was given the tour of the additional nursery first, which was decorated in lemon and blue and was utterly charming, as was the well-equipped mini kitchen stocked with enough baby formula to feed ten babies.

'It's all wired for sound,' the housekeeper explained

as she led her through to her own private sitting room, which was palatial in size and charmingly furnished with antique furniture, but nothing heavy or dark.

The bedroom, with its balcony, was dreamy with a four-poster and the same delightful feminine furniture, but it was her bathroom that stopped her in her tracks. Massive enough to dwarf the double-ended copper tub built for sharing, it boasted a stone fireplace complete with a wood burner, and a walk-in shower that had more touch buttons than a space module and a shower head the size of two dinner plates!

Setting Mattio's seat down on the marble floor, she sniffed a couple of the oils in the crystal flagons set along the matching marble shelf and turned on a tap in one of the twin sinks.

She could, she decided, picking up a fluffy towel from the top of one of the stacks, quite happily just live in here.

In the meantime, it was time to check out the kitchen for Mattio's feed.

'So, kiddo, what do you think of your place…not bad, hey?'

CHAPTER SIX

THE KNOCK ON the door pulled Maya away from the mirror. Did people actually dress for dinner outside movies and royal palaces? Where did castles fit into the scheme of things? Maya did have some experience of palaces and, though her sister had instigated a more casual approach since she'd taken up residence, when it came to family dinners at least, her life still involved a number of tiara occasions.

Luckily here Maya was not the hostess, family or a guest, in any proper sense of the word, so it was just as well she didn't possess a tiara or even a formal dress, at least not one she'd packed. She was normally a meticulous minimal packer and had not adapted well to the 'throw everything into a case in five minutes flat' approach.

But you worked with what you had, and her choice tonight had been between a good pair of jeans—aubergine velvet—an orange minidress she had worn once for a christening and a mid-length silk slip dress in a jewel-bright turquoise that could be dressed up or down.

The lack of jewellery to accessorise equated with dress-down, but the spiky-heeled ankle boots in a leopard print, which had involved the death of no leopards or, for that matter, any animals whatsoever, were definitely dress-up. They also made her appear quite tall, which although an illusion still felt quite nice.

She had worried when she'd first paraded in front of the massive ormolu framed mirror. True, the high neck of her dress revealed her collarbones, but nothing else. It was only when she turned around that you got the *wow* factor or, depending on your viewpoint, the *too much* factor. The back of the dress dipped dramatically almost to her waist and, while she *normally* didn't flinch from being slightly in your face clotheswise, tonight she had to admit to having some doubts.

Twisting around to look at her rear view, she frowned, then caught herself thinking, *What am I doing?*

Self-doubt was something she had left far behind her, and it had not been easy to do. She was no longer that person, the one who had felt as if she were fading into the background. It was no figure of speech—there had a point in her adolescence when she had *literally* felt almost invisible, thanks to evil Edward. Rediscovering her love of colour had been a visible reflection of how she felt inside—and how well she'd recovered from the abuse he'd heaped on her.

But there was bold and then there was all that

flesh… She solved this problem by leaving her hair loose so her exposed shoulder blades and all but the lowest section of the small of her back, just before the dip to her waist, were concealed beneath a curtain of curls ruthlessly tamed—with her hair there was no other way—by the brilliant product she had dragged through it with her fingers.

She took a deep breath, and pasted on a smile. She *could* do this, she'd just think of it as having a solo takeaway in front of the telly, except of course it wasn't either. It was the solo thing that bothered her most, which was insane. This categorically *wasn't* a dinner date, or for that matter any sort of date at all!

The woman on the other side of the door was young, more a girl, really, and was wearing the sort of informal uniform adopted by most staff that involved a white shirt and dark trousers.

Maya struggled to keep her smile in place as the girl's eyes widened in shock, doing a face-to-floor-and-back-again sweep. Her response was not *quite* a jaw-drop, but it came very close.

'Hello,' Maya said.

At the gentle prompt she flushed and rushed out, 'I am Rosa and I am here to sit with the little one.'

'Of course.' Maya stood back to allow the girl to enter the room. 'He's asleep.' She paused; it seemed ironic, considering the number of times she had been asked for ID to confirm her age, but this girl did look *very* young. 'Are you sure…?'

Rosa seemed to correctly interpret the hesitation to

hand over the care of the baby that Maya didn't totally understand herself.

'After school I worked in a pre-school nursery for a year. I begin my pre-nurse training at the university next month and I'm the eldest of seven.'

Which makes her much better qualified than me to take care of a baby, Maya mused wryly.

'Wow, that's, well… I've made a few notes for you if he wakes up.' She handed over the sheets she had jotted down some notes on.

'Thank you. Would you like me perhaps to get someone to show you down to the dining room…?'

It was an offer that Maya would have definitely appreciated had she not decided during the last ten seconds not to go down to the dining room at all.

'Actually, no, would it be possible for me to have a sandwich here?'

The girl looked confused.

'I'm feeling just a little tired and not so very hungry after all, so a sandwich in my room…that would be just fine.'

The girl tipped her head in compliance, very obviously struggling to hide the fact that she thought Maya was insane as she backed out of the room.

When the door closed, some of the tension left Maya's shoulders. She was, she told herself, totally comfortable with her choice.

It was important for her to believe it was a decision that had nothing to do with backing away from a challenge. It had been one of the things she had promised herself that she would never do once she had rebuilt her confidence one painful brick at a time after her stepfather had destroyed it with his insidious campaign— a person got told they were worth nothing on a daily basis and eventually they began to believe it.

She told herself that she had recovered fully from what had happened, but the questions Samuele had asked about her business hopes had shaken loose some uncomfortable possibilities she had been unconsciously avoiding. She did not regret refusing Beatrice and Dante's offers of assistance, but there were alternatives she could have taken. There were business loans available for new start-ups; she had done all the research into them, but at the last minute she had always backed away, telling herself that she didn't want to start out weighed down with debt. But she could see now the truth was that she was scared. Somewhere in the back of her mind she could still hear her stepfather telling her she was hopeless, useless.

It wasn't about pride or practicality; she was just scared, even if she hid it well.

And tonight? The strong reluctance to leave Mattio was totally genuine, and it had taken her by surprise, but wasn't there an element of her using it as an excuse not to spend the next couple of hours with Samuele?

In her defence, even if there was, she couldn't really be blamed; being around him was very exhausting because she couldn't lower her guard. She wasn't quite sure what she was guarding against, but she knew it was essential that she do so.

There were times when she decided to be brave and this wasn't one of them. Despite being more relaxed now she had made a decision—admittedly her jaw was still aching, but her teeth had unclenched—the static buzz of panic in her head had not gone away but it was less deafening.

Samuele would probably be relieved by her no-show. If he hadn't actually said that small talk wasn't really his thing, she felt it was a safe assumption to make, and she wasn't here to socialise anyway so starting as she meant to go on seemed a logical choice. In retrospect the entire 'what am I going to wear?', 'do I look good in this?', butterflies-in-the-stomach fizz of mingled excitement and anxiety was rather embarrassing, more suited to a date than what this was.

What was this?

She quickly gave up on finding a definition. It was far easier to say what it was not, and that was a date in any sense of the word.

She was just hoping that they were generous with the sandwiches because she had lied to Rosa—she was starving.

She wasn't really sure how long she'd been standing there lost in thought, but when the polite knock on the door came she still hadn't got around to kicking off her heels. Opening it wide ready to receive the tray—probably silver—she felt her smile fade and her hand drop to her side as she found herself facing not someone bearing a tray, but someone pushing a trolley, and another someone swiftly bringing up the rear.

'Oh, that is...' She gave a shrug, thinking it might not be a bad thing that there was wine when she spotted the cooler. She wasn't really much of a drinker but something to take some of the tension out of her shoulders would be good. 'Lovely,' she tacked on, stepping back to let them enter. It was easier than arguing and she wasn't about to send back good food when she was this hungry!

Hovering to helpfully close the door behind the waiters, who had their hands full, she found herself being pushed backwards as the door opened even wider to admit a tall figure. Her heart jolted.

Oh, dear, this wasn't going as planned!

Samuele had chosen to dress down but in a 'not as we know it' way, in black jeans that clung to his narrow hips and a pale blue linen shirt. Only a strong sense of self-preservation stopped her giving a little whimper of appreciation. It was the artist in her, she told herself. *The woman in her,* countered the voice in her head.

Samuele paused, registering her presence—how could a man not?—but resisting the very strong impulse to turn and stare. He conversed casually with the two staff members, delaying the moment just to prove to himself that he could. He was attracted to her, absolutely, but nothing had essentially changed; he was in perfect control of himself.

Maya was playing catch-up. Caught off guard by the sudden turn of events, her brain had lagged behind. The door was still open and she caught herself actually considering in a half-hearted joking way if anyone would notice if she just slipped away.

Man up, Maya, she told herself sternly. *You're the one who always says face your fears*—but her internal pep talk came to an abrupt halt when she realised she didn't want to know what she was afraid of.

Her eyes went to where Samuele stood looking impossibly handsome. He was smiling in response to something one of the waiters was saying, responding a moment later with a comment that made them both laugh. The informality she had noted since they'd arrived continued to surprise her; she had assumed that he'd be a remote authoritarian employer who demanded deference.

But then he didn't have anything to prove, did he? He had already their respect, so he didn't have to *demand* deference, it was just there. Watching the exchange made her think of the times when her stepfather would get huffy when people didn't use his full academic title.

She could remember squirming with embarrassment when he would speak over someone with a corrective *Professor* Edward Tyler.

In the time it took for her thoughts to slide through her head the small table beneath the window had been covered in a pristine white creaseless cloth, the finishing touches of crystal wine glasses and silver cutlery laid with geometric precision.

All impressive, but she barely noticed the crystal or silver; the thing that was registering with Maya was the fact they had laid two places. On one level she was aware that the light-headed fizz of excitement she was feeling at the thought of dining alone with Samuele in her suite was not an appropriate response.

She planted a hand against her throat, feeling the frantic pulse leap and twirl, and wondered if this was what a panic attack felt like, soothing herself with the reflection that even if it was it wasn't fatal—at least she didn't think so…

He turned, acknowledging her presence for the first time as the door closed behind his staff. 'I said we'd serve ourselves.' He offered the translation even though during her ridiculous panicking she had barely registered they were talking Italian.

'This is all…' she paused, clearing her throat as he reached for the bottle in the ice bucket. Popping the cork with a practised twist, he raised an interrogative brow and she hastily added faux-calmly, 'Very kind of you, but it's totally not… It isn't necessary.' She tried channelling a cool she was a million miles from feeling. 'I would have been fine with a sandwich,' she said, allowing her eyes to touch his but not making the mistake of maintaining eye contact.

'What? And leave you all dressed up and nowhere to go?'

He smiled slowly, and his eyes, as they swept up her body from her toes to her head, left a tingling trail of heat across her skin. 'You look lovely.'

She pulled in a tense breath and smiled nervously. 'I feel a bit overdressed.' *That* embarrassment she could shrug off; less easy was coping with the suffocating thud of her heartbeat, and the tingling sensation under her skin, as though a million butterflies were beating madly to get out.

Samuele was pretty sure he could have dealt with her overdressed problem in no time at all, but that would be playing with fire, so he closed down the visuals that went with the thought.

And you're not playing with fire already?

He closed down the inner voice too and dragged out a chair for her. He watched her hesitate before moving forward gracefully on those crazy heels, her slim thighs pushing against the silky jewel-bright fabric with each stride, forcing his pulse rate even higher. She looked sleek, sexy and exotic with her dark hair streaming like a glossy cloud down her back, just allowing him a peek of her naked lower back. The painful effort of not allowing the desire he felt to show on his face sent a trickle of sweat down his back.

What the hell are you doing here, Sam?

If his life was a roadmap, he felt that right at this moment he was standing at a crossroads. There were two paths ahead. He could see them perfectly clearly: one led to a businesslike short-term arrangement involving looking after Mattio for a few weeks, the other led straight to the bedroom.

One involved the short-term pain of self-denial, the other led to short-term, incredible pleasure... Ironically it was the degree of desire he felt to pursue the second option that made him hesitate. He'd already accepted that Maya was not the same as any other woman he had ever met.

Or was it just his own reactions to her that were different?

It wasn't just the utterly ridiculous level of attraction he was experiencing, it was *her*... *She* was different. When she was around he could not rely on the neat compartments that made his life run smoothly; nothing was contained.

He was so, so tempted to ignore the red warning signs in his head. If alcoholism ran in his family, he would have avoided alcohol; with his particular family history there were certain situations and women he avoided...and he certainly didn't need distractions in his life at the moment, as he focused on putting the last few pieces of the Agnosti estate back together. True, his work ethic had never stopped him having sex before, the difference being—he knew full well—that he had never had sex that touched his emotions.

And she already had, without them even kissing properly...but the admission came reluctantly. It had to be the same reason it had been almost *too* easy for him to open up and tell her such intimate, long-held secrets.

He was confident he *could* stay in control and have her at the same time, he would not admit to a weakness that suggested otherwise, but he didn't want to look at a woman when he left her, and see the shadows under her eyes and worry.

Who was he kidding? She had long-term relationship written all over her beautiful face! She would need things he didn't have to give because he had chosen his path in life. Loneliness was an infinitely preferable option to living his life being manipulated—and humiliated—by the woman he loved.

'I didn't expect this.' Maya paused, trying not to breathe in the clean masculine scent of him as she felt the warmth of his breath on her cheek. 'I just didn't want to be too far away from Mattio the first night we were here.' It was at least part of the truth; actually, it continued to amaze her every time she realised how deep the baby had burrowed his way into her heart so quickly.

Logic told her that it would be foolish to grow too fond of Mattio when very soon she would be walking away from him.

He wouldn't remember her, he was only a baby, but that didn't matter; she would still feel guilty when she left him, and she would always remember him.

Sadness filtered into her dark eyes as they lifted just as Samuele extended the wine bottle towards her glass. Unfortunately logic did not really play a part when it came to genuine emotions.

'No...yes,' she stuttered, struggling to keep the sudden rush of desperation from her voice as she removed her hand from the top of the crystal glass and pressed it close to her chest instead to hide the fact it was shaking; *she* was shaking.

Anyone would think you'd just made some sort of profound discovery, she mocked herself. *But you just fancy the man—it's hardly a shocking newsflash.*

Having never before felt a physical attraction this strong to any man, she could now see how some people mistook lust for something much more profound. But it was not a mistake she was about to make.

'Sorry to invade your space.' He looked around the room. 'Are you happy with your suite?'

'Absolutely.'

'And apologies again for the candles.' He cast an amused glance towards the lights flickering in the candelabra and gave a light laugh. 'I think my request to have dinner here with you was misinterpreted.'

Maya gave a laugh that she hoped sent the message that she had not for one moment misunderstood what this was. Absolutely *not* a date.

'I was thinking that dinner might be a good time to debrief one another each evening—would that work for you? Though obviously, should a problem arise re Mattio, I am available at any time. His well-being is my top priority.'

It was utterly irrational, given the circumstances, to feel chagrin. 'Of course, it is, and I have to eat,' she said, discovering her appetite had pretty much vanished despite the mouth-watering smells wafting towards her. 'So here's to the evening version of a working breakfast,' she said, raising the glass to her lips and taking a large mouthful.

She regretted now not taking the option of eating in more formal surroundings, not that the private lavish sitting room was exactly an intimate space. It was the company not the location that was the problem, she realised gloomily.

'My reputation would not survive if you leave here a shadow of your former self.'

'It all looks delicious,' she said brightly. 'But I'm afraid that there isn't much to report as yet. Mattio took his feed and he settled into his nursery pretty well. Do you want me to sleep in his room?' She had noticed the divan in the corner of the nursery.

No, I want you to sleep in my room. 'Of course not!' he snapped.

'Fine, I was only wondering—'

She stopped as his phone began to shrill, a look of annoyance crossing his face. 'Sorry, I meant to turn it off.'

'No problem.'

He glanced at the screen and grimaced. 'I have to take this.'

She shrugged and nodded.

His English was so syllable perfect, his accent barely there, that she had almost forgotten that it wasn't his first language. So when after listening for a few moments he launched into a heated diatribe in his native tongue she was jolted back to the reality of the situation.

Which was that he was Italian to his fingertips. Yes, he probably could make a shopping list sound sexy, but his sudden urgent passion as he spoke was utterly transfixing…in a stomach-quivering sort of way.

A few moments later he slid the phone back into his

pocket and, with a face like thunder, hammered out staccato fast what was presumably a shortened version of the conversation. In Italian.

She waited until he had finished, or at least paused to draw breath, to remind him quietly, 'You know I didn't understand a word you just said?'

He swore then in several languages and dragged a hand through his hair, ruffling the dark strands into toe-curlingly sexy spikes.

'Sorry, it's just that there are problems with one of our tenants. By the time my father died the place had been starved of resources for years, not to mention that there were entire areas where the trees had been razed... Ancient woodland raped for a quick profit.' The disgust in his voice was also etched in the bleak lines of his face, and his jaw was clenched so tight she could almost hear it grinding.

'Nothing replanted, land over-fertilised and the village was depopulated. There was nothing left for young people any more. A small investment meant ecotourism produced some almost immediate profit, but it's a long-term game. We'll start to see the benefits of the green approach soon, and in two years we might start to see some profit. Most of the tenants are on board with the plans but...' His expression darkened. 'There is a tenant who is not on board, for reasons I don't quite understand. He's not one of the old school, he is young and ambitious—exactly the sort of person I thought would be behind us.'

'But he isn't.'

'No, he isn't. There's an area of marshland which is important ecologically, as it's home to…' He paused and looked at her, suddenly seeming to remember who he was talking to. 'I'm so sorry, this must be boring you.'

'No, it isn't.' She was fascinated by this evidence of his connection to the land. 'It sounds like a difficult situation.'

'You could say that. I have been informed that some heavy machinery has arrived and his intention is to drain fifty acres of the marshland and put cattle on to graze. Apparently the concrete foundations for a barn arrives in the morning. Everything I'm working for will be destroyed for a quick profit. I have to go.' He got to his feet. 'I must stop this.'

Maya laid down her napkin and got to her feet and walked with him to the door. 'Well, goodnight.' She held out her hand. 'And good luck.'

He angled a sardonic dark brow. 'I'll probably need it—' The lights suddenly dimmed and went out completely, leaving the flickering candles as the only illumination in the room, highlighting the angles and planes of his face. 'Does this remind you of anything?' he murmured huskily.

Mesmerised by his dark stare, she nodded. 'The airport hotel. I wondered…'

'What did you wonder, *cara*?'

The words, uttered in a low gravelled tone, were almost like a physical caress. She swallowed. 'Did you kiss me?' she whispered.

He shook his head. In the semi-light his teeth were very white as he produced a slow smile, even while his eyes stayed dark and intent. Maya was too mortified to notice. Why, oh, why had she aired her fantasies out loud? Of course, he hadn't kissed her!

'No,' he confirmed. 'That was not a kiss.'

'Oh…?' she said, glad of the shadows to hide her embarrassed blushes.

He moved in a step and looked down into her face, murmuring something in Italian under his breath as his hand went behind her head. 'But this *is* a kiss.'

In the private theatre of Maya's thoughts and dreams he had already kissed her a thousand times, but this was different; it was so much better, it was *real*. Her initial pliant shock as she melted bonelessly into his arms suddenly gave way to a hunger that matched his own. One muscular arm banding her ribs, he lifted her feet off the floor as the kiss became more combative, more urgent.

Maya focused on not sliding to the floor as he placed her back on her feet and took a step back. She stared straight ahead, her eyes level with the middle of his heaving chest.

Yes, she had imagined what a kiss from him would be like, but it was nothing at all like that. She gave a wild little laugh. 'Yes, that was definitely a kiss. Oh, God!'

'Exactly.' His chest lifted in one last soundless jagged sigh before he turned and walked away with the sweet taste of Maya in his mouth.

CHAPTER SEVEN

SHE TENSED AT the tentative tap on the door, but only slightly. She didn't associate Samuele with tentative, so it was unlikely to be him. She had thought this morning might be awkward after their kiss, actually she had thought of spending the day in her bathroom, but it wasn't, because he didn't put in an appearance, and she ate her breakfast alone.

It had been a solitary sort of day. Maya had spent most of it in the nursery suite, although she had walked around a section of garden with Mattio in a pushchair, longingly eyeing up the extensive parkland and the oak woods beyond. She knew they were oak trees because she'd asked a gardener who was working outside. Their conversation had involved a lot of hand gestures, his English being only slightly better than her Italian, but she thought he'd understood her when she'd said she'd like to walk in the woods. There had been a moment when the communication had broken down and he had been particularly emphatic, saying *cinghiale*, and getting quite agitated, repeating it until in the end she'd nodded simply to soothe him.

Her visitor was Rosa, who would have been the babysitter of choice last night. Her English was excellent and Maya would have quite enjoyed a chat, but the girl was here to relieve her from baby duties. It was not presented as an option and the instructions had come directly from Samuele.

'Rafael will show you to the leisure suite. Do you swim?' Rosa asked.

'I don't have a costume.'

The girl gave a little giggle. 'There will be no one else there, but of course there are costumes available for when there are…guests, you understand.'

Maya did understand, of course she did, and she was instantly determined not to wear a swimsuit that had previously been worn by one of Samuele's female *guests*.

'You are not like them. I mean…'

Maya took pity on her confusion. 'I wouldn't mind an hour or so's break,' she admitted. 'But Mattio hasn't had a nap yet or—'

The girl dropped down beside the chair where the baby kicked his legs and continued to chew on a teething ring. 'Me and the bambino will be fine, you go, or I will be in trouble.'

Maya nodded and Rosa beamed. 'Shall I call Rafael?'

'No, it's fine, I'll find my own way.'

The girl looked doubtful. 'It is in the below part of

the castello, in the cellar. There are lifts, which are quite well hidden.'

'I'll be fine,' Maya promised.

Had she actually intended to take advantage of the pool she would have accepted the services of a guide. The castello was a warren of rooms and corridors and even making her way to the dining room for breakfast she had got turned around twice, but she intended to head outside to explore the oak woods and maybe even the vineyards beyond.

As she made her way through the parkland heading towards the wooded area she saw the elderly gardener in the distance and waved cheerily at him as he waved back enthusiastically.

It was good to be outside. She might have escaped the luxury of the castello, but the thoughts in her head were less easy to escape. She speeded up, ignoring the jeering voice in her head that was playing on a loop… *You can run but you can't hide.*

She didn't slow until she reached the trees. To her relief there was a definite pathway and she felt confident that she wouldn't get lost. The confidence began to ebb as the trees got denser and began to close in on her, but the path was still clear even though it was darker here, so she pushed on, breathing in the pungent scent of warm earth underfoot. Several times she imagined she heard rustling, and once a flicker of movement in the periphery of her vision but, peering through the branches, she saw nothing.

She was actually on the point of turning back when

the trees began to thin and the path opened up into a small clearing. She let out a small cry of delight, and had crouched down to examine the tiny flowers that carpeted the floor when she heard a snap of twigs and a snuffling sound.

She froze, this time knowing it was definitely not her imagination. She wasn't alone.

'Is somebody there?' *What are you going to do if someone says yes?* that voice jeered again.

Run!

She huffed out a laugh of sheer relief when out of the undergrowth a little pig appeared, furry and ginger with stripes down its back. Utterly charmed, she rose to her feet and approached it slowly so as not to frighten it. 'Hello there, little one, are you lost? Ooh, hello there as well,' she added, moving forward, her hand outstretched as three more of the cute creatures appeared, making little whining noises.

She reached into her pocket to find her phone, as she had to have a photo of these, when a loud grunting and squealing behind her made her jump. She almost dropped the phone as she spun around expecting to see more piglets.

She froze. This was not a cute creature, though it might once have been. She knew she was looking at the adult version, and a prickle of fear made the hairs on the nape of her neck stand on end. The tiny eyes gave it a mean look as it stared at her past its long, hard snout, and the piglets started squealing even louder.

The parent—mother?—started forward, letting out another angry snorting noise.

Samuele was petrified. 'Do not run, Maya,' he said as quietly as he could, struggling with the image in his head of her being run down within seconds.

Maya was frozen to the spot.

'I can't.'

'Oh, *cara*, you can,' he insisted softly, cold sweat slicking his skin as he watched her poised like a gazelle about to run. 'Now, don't make any sudden noise but start to back away from her very slowly.'

She began to turn her head to look at him. 'No!' His voice dropped back to a low, soft, soothing monotone as he emphasised, 'Do not turn around or look at me, just keep moving backwards, perfect, perfect… very slowly…'

She clung to his voice like a lifeline, each calm yet emphatic syllable stopping her succumbing to total panic.

'Samuele…'

'You will be fine, I promise. I won't let anything happen to you, but be careful and do *not* fall over.' He had seen the damage a female wild boar could do in defence of her young; she might lack the tusks of the male, but she was fast and those teeth could inflict some wicked wounds. The idea of them tearing into Maya's flesh filled him with a fear that was visceral in its intensity.

One of the piglets rushed towards Maya and he

clenched his teeth against a groan as the mother's angry squeals intensified—she was going to charge.

Without taking his eyes from the animal he reached down for the fallen branch his boot was balanced on.

'Maya.'

She was shaking, her chalk-white pale face dotted with beads of cold sweat. Being paralyzed with fear had taken on an entirely new meaning.

'Can you hear me?'

'Yes,' she whispered.

'You are going to do what I tell you, when I tell you and not before…do you understand?'

She nodded. 'Yes.'

'Good girl. There is a track behind you and to the left—it goes uphill. I want you to run, but not until I say. Run and don't look back, don't stop until you reach the observatory.'

'The what?'

'You will know when you're there.'

'What about you?'

'I will be fine if you do what I ask you to.' The rustle as he tightened his hand over the branch turned the boar's mean red eyes his way, and she began to move away from Maya. 'That's it, come over here, Mama Boar. Now get ready, Maya.' He lifted the branch and banged the ground, yelling like a banshee, the infuriated animal charged and he shouted, 'Now, Maya! Run, *cara*, run!' He waited just long enough to see that she had taken off before he hit the ground running, still yelling as he did so.

There was no way he could outrun an enraged boar who, despite her bulk, could really move, and he knew that his only chance was getting high enough up… once he was sure that Maya was far enough away from those teeth.

Maya ran, her heart pumping, self-preservation giving her feet wings as she ran, instinct rather than a recollection of his instructions putting her on the right path. Panting tears sliding down her cheeks, she ran on uphill, stumbling over roots but knowing that she could not fall… She barely noticed when a stray overhanging branch delivered a glancing blow to her cheek. More tears blurred her vision as she refused to look back— *don't look back, and don't fall*.

Her lungs felt as though they would burst when the trees cleared quite abruptly and she saw her goal. The small, square stone building with the domed roof of glass was an incongruous sight, but she wasn't asking why it was there. She was only focused on the sanctuary offered by the metal-banded doors, thinking… *Not locked, please, not locked!*

It wasn't.

One side of the double doors opened without any effort on her part as she slipped inside the sanctuary and closed it fast behind her. She leaned against it, eyes closed and shaking with reaction, her laboured breathing gradually slowing.

Oh, God…Samuele!

Her eyes flew wide and she turned and pushed the

doors she had just closed open again. She was sobbing again, loudly, but she didn't hear as she was seeing him banging the ground with his stick, deliberately drawing the vicious animal to him... She had left him, deserted him, *abandoned* him; she was *that* person, the person she despised.

If he was harmed she would never forgive herself.

Self-disgust settled over her like a black cloud as she waited, her eyes trained on the woods, alert to any sign of sound or movement. If he was hurt or worse it was on her.

He could be lying out there slashed and bleeding, needing help. She became so convinced by the lurid images in her head that she had just made the decision to go out and find him when he appeared.

She didn't immediately see him, just a movement in the periphery of her vision. She had been willing him to appear, but he came from a totally different direction.

The relief was so intense she thought she was going to faint, then she realised the faintness was probably associated with the fact she was hyperventilating.

Consciously slowing her breathing, she took a step towards him.

'You're not dead!' Even as she spoke it crossed her mind that she had never seen anyone look more alive. His eyes were burning bright, the glitter in them almost incandescent, though one leg of his trousers was ripped from the ankle almost to the thigh, revealing olive-tanned hair-roughened skin and long slabs of muscle.

There were scratches on his face, some oozing blood, but he looked totally relaxed as he drew level with her and he wasn't even breathing hard. It struck her that he looked more dangerous than the boar.

A danger that anyone with a pinch of sense would run away from, but his hands lay heavy on her shoulders and she couldn't have run even if she had wanted to, which she didn't.

'Dead?' He laughed and shook his head. 'The *cinghiale* rarely kill but they can cause some serious damage and ugly scars. Some hunters say boars are more dangerous than bears, though we don't have any of those here.' His white grin appeared. 'Just wolves.'

He was giving her a natural history lesson! She had been half out of her mind and he was telling her it wasn't so very bad...*cinghiale*...why was that Italian word ringing bells?

Sam's eyes moved swiftly across her face, noting the bruise developing on her cheek, his jaw quivering as he felt a twisting sensation in his chest, a tenderness that he was reluctant to name.

'You did good,' he said roughly, releasing her.

'I did,' she agreed breathlessly.

Her eyes widened, and she stood there visibly trembling as he reached out again. She stayed statue-still, her eyes connected with his, swaying slightly as his fingers pushed into her hair, lightly grazing her scalp.

He felt her shiver and watched the pupils of her eyes

dilate, the longing in her eyes… It was hard to not see
danger when it was literally staring you in the face.

It was just seeing her here safe and sound, the relief, the elation after the not knowing, the nightmare
scenarios that had been going through his head while,
Madre di Dios, he'd been trapped up a tree until that
damned boar had finally given up the hunt.

They were all good reasons for the way he was
feeling but not excuses… Control…he needed control.

'Got it! Did you leave any forest out there?' he
asked, opening his hand to reveal the twig he'd gently
pulled out of her hair before he dropped it and ground
it underfoot, his eyelashes lowering to hide the burning desire in his eyes.

The anticlimax was as shocking as a slap, and the
subsequent mood change as dramatic as it was intense.
She wanted to cry again, and she could actually feel
the tears pressing at the backs of her eyes. You're in
shock, she told herself, glad to put a name to the roller
coaster of emotions and her heightened mood.

'You found it, then.'

He was looking past her, and she turned her head,
not even pretending an interest as her glance moved
through the open doors of the observatory to the interior. She was seeing the cedar-lined walls within for
the first time, hung round with bookcases and with a
sumptuous day bed just to the right of the spiral staircase. From where they stood, she could see just make
out the glass dome above the telescope set in a mez-
zanine observation platform.

'My grandfather was a stargazer. Actually, he was quite a well-respected amateur astronomer, so he restored the observatory and—'

'You enjoyed it, didn't you?' Maya interrupted ruthlessly. She could feel the emotions building up inside her, feel the pounding in her temples like a hammer hitting a crumbling wall…each thud destroying more of the mortar and her self-control.

He recognised the antagonism shining in her eyes, but he didn't really understand it. He hadn't exactly enjoyed the heart-pumping run here, seeing as every step had been burdened by the *not knowing*, the fear eating away at him that she might have been hurt. Every second he'd had to spend up that damn tree not knowing if she was all right had felt like a century, so when he'd seen her standing there unharmed it had felt like… He actually had nothing to compare the feeling to, it was way more complex than anything he could imagine, but perhaps akin to the sheer elation you felt when you emerged from the icy water after wild swimming.

'Well, it's always good to get the better of a boar,' he responded calmly, sticking to facts, not feelings. 'The thing to remember is you can't outrun them, so don't try. Your best bet is to climb a tree. I did,' he admitted, working on the theory that while he was talking he couldn't be kissing her, and he wanted to, he really wanted to… He needed to taste her, and the greedy need was hampering his ability to frame coherent sentences. 'They are incredibly destructive beasts. They cause total havoc. Last year they took over a thousand gallons of grapes and it's virtually impossible to keep them out. We put down miles of electric fences around the vineyards but they just jump them, and I'd take the tusks of a male over the protective instincts of a female any day.'

'You think I want a natural history lesson?'

He bent in, struggling to catch her quiet words, but a second later he was leaning back out again, because he had no problem hearing the next thing she said— they probably heard her in the village five miles away.

'You were enjoying yourself beating the piglets in some macho game while I,' she shouted, stabbing a straight finger hard into his chest, 'I,' she repeated with another stab into his muscular chest, 'I thought you were dead!' she shrieked. 'And it was my fault.'

The fight left her without warning; her legs sagged and she would have slid to the floor had the arm wrapped around her ribs not taken the weight. She looked up at him through the overflow of luminous tears that started to seep out from the corners of her eyes.

'You're crying…' Samuele really didn't know how to deal with the protective surge he felt as he watched the tears silently slide down her cheeks.

'No, I'm not,' she denied fiercely, as though he had insulted her by caring.

Fine, he thought, adopting a heart-of-stone expression, although it was incredibly hard when she looked so fragile…so sexy. 'You're in shock.'

Maya wanted to lash back and tell him he had no idea what she was feeling, only neither did she.

The beginnings of a bewildered frown froze in place as he reached out and cupped her face, his fingers cool on her skin. His expression was fierce his concentration total as he followed the path of his thumb as he slid it across the red mark that stood out against the smooth skin of her cheek.

'Sorry,' he said, clearly misinterpreting her shiver. 'You were very stupid—'

She could not in all honesty deny this.

'And very, very brave…' He brought his face in close, his nose grazing hers, his breath warm on her cheek. 'You are driving me totally crazy, you know,' he rasped, ignoring the voice in his head that told him he was finally losing control of the situation, losing control of himself.

Why bother fighting? said that wicked voice of temptation in his head. *Just relax, enjoy it while you can…*

His face was so close Maya couldn't focus, so she closed her eyes and felt his lips against her eyelids.

'Look at me!'

She responded to the fierce command at the same moment he settled his mouth on hers, the sensuous pressure drawing a whimper from her throat, then, when his tongue slid across the outline of her lips, she grabbed hold of his shirt in handfuls just to stop from sliding to the ground. His lips were cool but she could feel the primal heat coming off him in waves, smell the musky scent of arousal.

Shocked by the fist of need in her belly and the surge of desire that was tangled in with a mess of emotions, she reached up instinctively, her arms curling around his neck, pulling him down to her while arching upwards, wanting…wanting more… Reacting with a fierce little gasp of shock to the very explicit proof of his arousal as she felt the imprint of his erection grinding into her belly.

She was plastered against him, but then with no warning at all the sensual connection was broken and the heat was gone as he physically put her away from him, the only warmth his big hands that still spanned her waist.

'You understand that this is just sex, right, Maya?' He'd never slept with a woman where the warning had been needed, because they'd always understood the game; he'd never needed to hear the words to give himself permission to continue, either. It was just sex, he reiterated to himself, panic bolting through him as he imagined her saying no to his question, because she wanted more from him. Because he couldn't give her more.

The more she totally deserves, taunted the voice of guilt pricking at his conscience.

His eyes were dark and smoky, his skin when she placed a hand flat on his chest was hot too… This was not a rejection, she understood that; it was just him laying out the rules before they started.

As she had never had sex before, she doubted she would notice the difference between that and…anything more. *Just sex,* he'd called it. But it wasn't as though she'd asked him for more, was it?

Not as if she deserved more!

Not as if she deserved love.

No wonder your biological mother rejected you…

'What is it?' he asked, watching the expressions flicker across her lovely face and feeling a rush of protective emotion that was so intense he felt as though someone had reached inside his chest and squeezed his heart.

She shook her head and smiled, feeling suddenly liberated. She would *not* allow Edward to spoil this moment or any other moment for her. She was not a child any longer with no self-esteem and Samuele was not trying to diminish her, he was only being honest.

'I was just remembering something someone used to say to me.'

Her stepfather had been so clever at locating a weak spot and exploiting it. He'd clawed at the one tiny shadow inside her heart that still grieved because she'd been abandoned by her own mother, and by the time he'd finished with her, she had carried an echo of that fear into adulthood. It had prevented her having any intimate relationships because she was afraid of being rejected, for being made to feel like that little girl who didn't deserve love.

'I will make you forget him, *cara.*'

She smiled. 'I've already forgotten. I want you, Samuele, you are exactly what I need right now.'

A low growl was released from his throat as the last shreds of control he had placed himself under snapped.

It felt as though she were being swept away by a fast-flowing river as his mouth came crashing down on hers; his grip on her waist tightened as he lifted her up against his tense, hard length. Not thinking through her actions, because she was deep in instinct territory now, she wound her arms around his neck, sinking her fingers into the hair on his nape and kissing him back hard as her legs wrapped tightly around his waist to hold herself there.

He broke off the kiss long enough to give a fierce grin as he slid his hands beneath her bottom and they stumbled the few steps to the stone building.

On the receiving end of Samuele's deep, drugging, sense-shredding kisses, she barely registered him kicking the door closed behind them, but she knew that they were alone and common sense, along with the rest of the world, was locked outside.

Samuele pushed aside all the plump scatter cushions on the day bed with one sweep of his hand. He sat down on the upholstered edge and Maya, with her legs still around his waist, landed sitting on his lap.

Her head had slid to his shoulder and he hooked a thumb beneath her chin and tilted her face up to his. He could see that her eyes were big and unfocused, the velvety pansy-brown glazed with passion.

With an almost feral groan he kissed her hard,

lowering her back onto the day bed, which was wide enough to accommodate them both side by side, but he fell on top of her, a knee braced either side of her body. He pulled himself up just far enough to free his shirt from his jeans and fumbled with the belt. Clenching his teeth with frustration at the delay, he tore at the buttons on his shirt, before tugging at his zip, giving only partial relief from the painful constriction.

Maya placed her hand flat against the ridges of his belly. Simultaneously shocked and excited by the hardness and heat of his skin, she grabbed the loose ends of his belt and tugged. He resisted, drawing a cry of protest from her aching throat that faded into a whimper as he took the edges of the long-sleeved T-shirt she wore and pulled it over her head.

She didn't have the strength or the will to move her hands, so they still lay splayed above her head in an attitude of submission. Her breath, coming as a series of uneven shallow gasps, snagged on a moan as he slid the straps of her bra over her shoulders, massaging and kissing the skin stretched across the angle of her collarbones before he traced a moist path down the valley between her breasts with his tongue.

He lifted himself off her just enough to fight his way clear of his shirt, and she came up on her knees to help him, kissing his chest as it was revealed, tasting the salt in his sweat as she slid her hands over his golden skin.

Her bra of tartan satin followed his abandoned shirt, sailing somewhere over her head as he threw it away.

'*Dio!*'

The peaks of her breasts hardened and tingled under his scrutiny. She arched at the first touch of his hand and fell back onto the day bed, gasping, at this, their first intimate, skin-to-skin contact. She twisted and squirmed against him as her small hands went to the half-open zip of his jeans. She struggled with it until he rolled away and, lifting his hips off the bed, peeled the jeans off along with his boxers. He snatched his wallet from his jeans pocket, before kicking his clothes away until they fell with a thud and clatter on the other side of the room.

Maya swung her legs over the side of the bed and unfastened her cotton pedal pushers. She stood up for a moment to pull them down over her hips and step out of them.

Turning, she reached up to find Samuele's hands curling around her upper arms, knowing as he found his eyes on her, devouring the abandoned look of her, that it was an image that would stay with him for ever. Her skin was like silk, her body as beautiful as her face, and he knew she was a perfect fit for him.

She *was* perfect and utterly oblivious to the fact, too. There was nothing feigned about her natural sensuality that made her every move provoking and exciting to Samuele.

She made him feel utterly insatiable… He drew her to him, greedy to touch her everywhere, feel her, explore the smooth softness of her slender, toned body, unable to imagine ever having enough of her.

Lying on top of him, Maya could feel the deep ripples of his muscles as she touched him, exploring the hard counters of his body. Surrendering to the urgency that was burning her up from the inside out, she revelled in the freedom he was giving her to express herself, the lack of any boundaries, as his hands and mouth were everywhere, drawing gasps and moans from her.

When he asked her what she liked she told him with breathless honesty.

'Everything…every part of you.'

His control broke and then she was beneath him, her legs parted, as he teased her with the pressure of his erection against her damp mound until finally he couldn't hold out any longer. Grabbing a packet from his wallet, he sheathed himself quickly and surged smoothly into her.

The pleasure that rushed through her as he entered her drew a deep moan of ecstasy from her lips. Gasping and trembling with an overload of feeling, she reached up and kissed him on his mouth before trailing her tongue along the damp corded skin of his throat.

Then it began in earnest, the slow delicious torment of his fluid, sensuous advance and retreat. The intimacy of being joined with him was like nothing she had imagined it could be; she could literally *feel* the thudding of his heart against her own. Having him inside her felt so incredibly *right*, and with each thrust he touched a part of her that no one had ever touched before, winding her tighter and tighter until she felt as if she were going to explode into a million stars.

She opened her eyes and saw the raw naked need in his eyes; it was like looking into a mirror and seeing exactly what she felt on someone else's face.

The sudden intensity of her release was shocking, like free falling without a parachute but with no impact, just waves and waves of bone-deep drowning pleasure that was better than even the most vivid of her dreams…

CHAPTER EIGHT

MAYA SLOWLY FLOATED back down to earth. There was sound and light, and she could see an expanse of blue through the incredible domed glass ceiling.

What would it be like to just lie here with your lover and do nothing except make love under this roof of stars? Well, she didn't have a lover and she hadn't made love either. She'd just had sex, and now it was over.

He rolled away from her and as she looked at his sweat-slicked face through the veil of her lashes she could see that the distancing was not just physical.

Was it wrong to want to prolong the moment, hold on to the image of delicious warm intimacy for a little while longer, even if it wasn't real? Well, it was what she wanted, even though she knew a clean break would be less painful, so she closed her eyes and went for the masochistic option.

Not that she had any room for complaint. This was exactly what she had signed up for and she'd do it again in the blink of an eye.

As her breathing gradually slowed, she knew there

was probably a *'You should have told me'* coming, but she wanted to both delay the moment…and stretch out this moment at the same time.

It said something about her day when discovering an observatory in the middle of a forest was the least surprising thing that had happened to her!

She turned her head and looked into the eyes of the most surprising thing. His expression was veiled, and it didn't alter even when she reached out and laid her hand on his chest, feeling the thud of his heart through her fingertips, still wanting to keep a connection, any connection, between them.

'I keep thinking, what if you hadn't been in the woods at exactly the moment that I stumbled across the boar?'

He looked at her sharply and gave a harsh laugh that faded quickly. 'Stumbled,' he echoed. 'You think it was a lucky coincidence or fate maybe?'

'Wasn't it?'

'No, it was not. It was because old Santino nearly gave himself a heart attack running to get help,' he said grimly. 'The only coincidence involved was him bumping into me first. He was totally desperate. He said you were going into the woods even though he had warned you about the boars, and explained how dangerous the females were when they had litters in this season, and how one boar had killed his dog last year.'

The gruesome details made her flinch. 'The *gardener*, Santino?'

'Yes, the gardener, Santino. How could you be so

foolish, so arrogant, as to ignore his warning and put yourself in danger like that?' He'd been so angry, he'd intended to shake her when he found her; instead he'd made passionate love to her.

'But he doesn't speak much English and I...oh, God...*cinghiale*. He was warning me. I didn't understand. I just pretended to because he seemed so upset.' There was a slightly hysterical sound to her laughter, and she had to literally bite her tongue to stop it.

Beside her Samuele had gone very quiet; he had rolled onto his side, and now he lay propped on one elbow looking down at her. She refused to meet his eyes, because she knew exactly what was coming.

And it came, although his voice was not as cold as she'd expected; it was totally neutral, which was somehow worse.

Samuele had to force himself to unclench the muscles in his jaw so he could speak. 'You know that can't happen again, Maya,' he said. Inside his head, he was thinking, *You knew it shouldn't have happened even once, Sam! Virgin, she'd been a virgin!* God, this was utter madness. He'd used the *'This is just sex'* line on her as though it were some sort of magic talisman that let him break his self-imposed rule about sleeping with her, and now look what had happened!

'Why didn't you tell me I was your first?'

Maya sighed, retracting the hand that had still been touching his hair-roughened thigh, and finally met his penetrating gaze. 'It wasn't relevant.' She felt him stiffen and saw the outrage flare in his eyes…which jolted her temper into life.

'It was *my* choice who I slept with first, Samuele. Mine. When, where and with whom, and I made my choice. I don't think I owe you any explanations, do I? Because, like you said, it was just sex and that happens to suit me perfectly.'

'I don't believe you,' he said flatly.

She saw no reason at all to give him the psychological advantage of being the one looking down on her, so she sat up in one fluid motion, with only her tangled dark curls to hide behind.

If things had been different she might have felt self-conscious about being naked, but ironically lovemaking with the patently enthusiastic Samuele had made her even more confident about her body, and anger, which she had fully embraced by now, was a very good antidote to shyness.

'Fine. So you were present for the most important moment of my life. Is that what you want me to say?' She rolled her eyes but didn't quite meet his—that would have required better acting skills than she possessed. She even delivered a laugh, hiding the truth inside a joke and a series of increasingly desperate lies. 'Look, maybe you think every woman you meet is looking for love, but me, I'm not. I'm actively avoiding it. I mean, why should you be the only one?'

Through the veil of her lashes she could see the jibe had found its mark, and she felt a stab of bleak satisfaction. 'Virtually everyone I have ever cared for, and even those I didn't, have abandoned me at some point in my life. Why would I set myself up for even more pain by falling in love?' she pointed out, embracing what she had never admitted to herself before and feeling weirdly liberated because of it. 'My own mother rejected me—*twice*, actually, when you think about it. She clearly never loved me, and neither did Violetta.' Sadness filled her face as she admitted quietly, 'My dad died when I was only a child and I was devastated because I loved him so much. My mum remarried and—well, let's just say you're certainly not the only person who's seen a parent make a terrible second marriage. What did love do for her? And while my sister Beatrice is happy now, she went through absolute hell to get there.

'*She* thinks love is a price worth paying, but *I* don't. My mum and dad were blissfully happy for a few short years but when he died, I think a part of her did too, and she ended up marrying a man on the rebound who was a total control freak. He tried and almost succeeded in isolating her from everyone who cared for her, and he practically ripped our family apart doing it.

'The truth is, I owe you a sincere debt of gratitude, Samuele.' She saw surprise move at the backs of his eyes and felt a stab of triumph. 'I thought that I couldn't have sex without a relationship, that it would feel cold and wrong. But it didn't, and it was incredible. So you have opened up a whole new world of possibilities for me.'

He isn't rejecting me—I'm rejecting him... She repeated the confidence-enhancing mantra inside her head over and over. It didn't matter if it was true, because it was always about how it *looked* rather than how it actually *was*, and she looked totally confident as she surged gracefully to her feet. Displaying an almost balletic poise, she moved around the room, unhurriedly gathering her clothes.

It was hard to project dignity while you were untangling your bra from a lampshade, especially when you could feel a pair of jet-dark eyes following your every move, but Maya thought she pulled it off. Cool and businesslike might have been preferable, and she might well have said more than she'd intended to about her past, though the details of her big speech were already a bit of a blur. But what she *had* done was establish that she was *not* crushed by his declaration that he wouldn't sleep with her again. Because she was his equal. Actually, she decided, she was *better* than him.

Sam watched as she turned her back to him and he had a last flash of her small, high, coral-tipped breasts that had fitted so perfectly into his hands before she covered them with the tartan silk bra. Then she pushed her hair out of the way, drawing it over her shoulder to gain access to the fastening.

The Pre-Raphaelite mass of curls always made him think of an old film… He remembered it being themed rather appropriately around a young woman with incredible hair who discovered her sexuality, a view and the Italian scenery all at the same time.

Well, Maya had certainly discovered her sexuality,

he thought grimly, and now she was going to be exploring it with someone else. The image of these faceless
recipients of her loving sensuality sent a knife thrust
of something acidic that he *refused* to admit was pure,
undiluted jealousy.

Recognising the source of the feeling in his gut
when he imagined someone else pushing his face into
her hair, breathing in the scent of her, of that someone feeling the brush of the silky cascade against his
chest and belly, exciting nerve-endings into painful
life, would be to admit to a vulnerability that he was
unwilling to own.

Pushing away the images, he rose to his feet, watching the flexing of her shoulder blades cause a little
ripple of delicately sculpted muscle under the surface
of her creamy skin.

'I need to get back to Mattio now.' Maya tossed the
information over her shoulder, feeling a stab of shame
that he was her only reason for being here, and yet
she'd so easily forgotten her responsibilities.

As the fastener clicked home and she was able to
drop her arms, she turned to see him standing there
stark naked. Her mood of defiant confidence slipped
away as she stared, literally transfixed by the sight of
him. There was not an ounce of surplus fat beneath
his olive-toned skin to disguise the delineation of his
athletic frame, the deep muscles on his long thighs, the
powerful muscles of his broad shoulders and chest, and
the washboard corrugation of his belly.

Things newly awoken inside her tightened and

clenched. Who was she kidding? Samuele had not opened her up to a world of sensual possibility, he had just *spoilt* her for any other man! She couldn't even bear to contemplate the idea of another man touching her as intimately as he had...

'Mattio will be fine,' he said quietly. 'And you will be a celebrity once everyone knows what happened.'

The colour slid from her face. 'You're going to tell them?'

'You will, I would imagine.'

She stared at him. Why would she tell everyone she'd slept with Samuele?

'The bruise on your face is going to take some explaining if you don't tell them about the boar.'

She reached for her shirt then, crushing it to her front as she felt the wash of embarrassed colour rise up her neck. She would have died rather than admit the misunderstanding.

He watched her from under his lashes as he pulled his jeans up over his narrow hips, knowing the conclusion she'd just jumped to. Boast about sleeping with a virgin? Ignorance, in his mind, was no defence; he certainly wasn't going to expose his shame. It didn't matter which way you looked at it, he had the experience, and he'd made a move on her when she'd been at her most vulnerable, shocked and upset after almost being badly injured.

The terrible truth was that he would do it again in a heartbeat...and now he knew that Maya Monk could very quickly become his drug of choice, the only option was to go cold turkey. It disturbed him that for the first time in his life his contempt for his father, his despair for his brother, both locked into marriages that amounted to contractual humiliation, was now leavened with the smallest kernel of understanding. Not that Maya bore any resemblance to his toxic stepmother…but that only made her more dangerous to him, not less.

Having her under the same roof as him for several weeks might be a challenge, but maybe he deserved to suffer after what he'd done? Keeping an emotional distance from her wasn't going to be painless either.

'I'll go first,' he said as she walked through the door ahead of him.

'Because you're big and male and I'm a weak little woman?' she jibed.

No, because I can't take looking at your delicious rear all the way back without wanting to have you up against the nearest tree. He shrugged. 'If you like.'

Even though he didn't turn around he must have sensed her hesitation as they approached the trees again. 'Don't worry, that family of boars have probably moved on,' he lied. In actuality he didn't have a clue if they had or not. He'd protect Maya even if he had to pick her up and run all the way back to the castello with her.

'No, it's not that. It's just…you saved my life and I didn't say thank you.'

He paused and looked back over his shoulder. 'I think you said thank you very nicely indeed. In fact, it was one of the nicest thank-yous I have ever received, *cara*.'

He winked at her, then watched the angry colour stain her cheeks. He turned away thinking, *Job done*. Having her angry with him was no bad thing. He resolutely ignored the hollow feeling in his stomach.

CHAPTER NINE

IT WAS TWO weeks and the bruise on her cheek had almost faded. She had woken the next day to find she had a black eye and her face had gone through some lurid colour changes since then; now a light touch of concealer and you wouldn't know it was there.

If only other things that had happened that day had faded so easily…though a part of her didn't actually want them to. Samuele had been right: her encounter with the wild boars had made her a bit of a local celebrity.

She had a lot of sympathy and was repeatedly told how lucky she was. It seemed everyone had a story of someone who hadn't been as lucky: the hiker who had nearly lost an eye and had been massively disfigured; the farmhand who had fallen and been trampled coming out of his encounter with several broken ribs and a smashed leg…he still walked with a limp, she was told darkly.

Maya had made a point of going out to the gardens to search out the gardener and offer her thanks

and apologies. She took Rosa with her to translate and
showed Santino the app on her phone she would use
to translate for herself in future.

She stayed and won a friend by asking about the
gardens that he and his team kept so beautifully, and
he was eager to tell her about the years when he had
been the only one left to tend them and how it had
simply broken his heart to see the historically important landscapes being taken over by Mother Nature.

'Now,' he proudly explained, 'I have every resource
I ask for and a team.' He spoke at length about last
summer and the massive party with famous people and
the filmmaker who had wanted to make a documen-
tary about the gardens. 'The son,' he finished, crypti-
cally tapping his nose. 'He is nothing like the father...'

It was the first time she'd heard this opinion actually voiced, but it was implied in so many other con-
versations she had had. Samuele was more than simply
well regarded; he was flat-out adored by the people
of the estate.

She wondered what the high-flying financiers in
their smart suits—not that any of them filled out a
suit like Samuele—would make of the man she had
seen last week?

Her thoughts drifted back to her solo walk she'd
fitted into her daily routine, which no longer involved
intimate dinners with Samuele. Sometimes Rosa, who
had become her official helper with Mattio, stayed to
eat with her, which involved far less tension.

Maya's walk that particular morning last week had

taken her past the stables. She was a bit nervous of horses, or at least the height they were from the ground, so she had been far enough away to stay unseen, or at least that was what she had thought until that final moment when Samuele had turned and looked directly at her. To her eternal shame she had ducked down behind a hedge, a bit like a child who covered his eyes and thought no one could see him.

Only she wasn't a child and she had sat there and sworn under her breath, waiting for her humiliation to be complete when he came over—but he hadn't.

While it had lasted, the show she'd seen had been quite a masterclass in horsemanship; if anyone had filmed it on their phone it would have gone viral in hours!

How could it not? It had everything: a tall, gorgeously handsome man radiating authority standing there, seemingly oblivious to the slashing hooves of the young horse he was trying to tame.

Maya's initial gut-chilling fear had given way to fascination as she'd watched him. It had been like a ballet really, the horse advancing and retreating and Samuele standing there completely unfazed, radiating the sort of confidence that you couldn't learn or fake or buy, and gradually, almost by osmosis, it had seemed to infiltrate the animal's panic.

She hadn't been the only one watching the show, the fence had been lined with stable hands who had seemed as fascinated as she'd been.

Samuele hadn't appeared to *do* anything except talk

softly. Nothing had happened fast but by imperceptible inches he'd won the horse's trust until he was able to stroke his silky face, after which he'd trotted around the exercise ring quite happily.

That was when he'd turned and looked at her; that was when she should have walked calmly over to him and said something bland, talked about the weather, anything but what she'd done.

She still cringed when she thought about what she must have looked like.

Would he comment on it this morning? she wondered, gathering up the folder containing the nannies' CVs and sticking it into her shoulder bag. She assumed that that was why he had requested her presence this morning, via email, which had been the form of communication he had favoured since they'd had their… sexual collision. It was how she'd decided to think of it, like a traffic accident that had happened because you hadn't been paying attention to the road, or because you'd allowed yourself to think about something else instead, like him, standing naked in front of you… Which wasn't going to happen today, she told herself firmly.

It would be their first meeting that wasn't accidental in two weeks. They'd occasionally passed one another in one or other of the maze of corridors and once she had been going into the magnificent leisure suite when he'd been coming out, his hair wet… She'd felt dizzy for quite a while after that. A few minutes earlier and she would have seen him sleek and semi-naked in the pool, maybe even joined him there…? Then who knew what might have happened? Her vivid imagination had supplied several possibilities in glorious Technicolor.

She had not ventured back there since.

Their paths had almost crossed a few times when he'd come to see Mattio, but each time he had she'd been taking her walk and Rosa had been in charge. The girl had given her chapter and verse of how good he was with the baby and how interested he was in Mattio's progress.

Maya couldn't decide what was worse: the possibility he was avoiding her, or he'd forgotten she existed and moved on.

Another one of his personal secretaries, the woman, appeared as Maya approached the office door. Maya suspected that being psychic was probably a required qualification for working closely for Samuele—that and an inbuilt immunity to his intellect-dampening aura of raw masculinity.

That disqualified her on both counts. She was almost as miscast as an employee as she was a lover, even though technically she wasn't either. She'd just been a steamy one-afternoon stand for him, and, far from feeling as if she worked for him, she was actually treated more like a guest by everyone she encountered here. Everyone except the boss, who acted as though she were invisible. Yes, it suited her too, but she didn't have to be happy about it, did she?

'Just give him a minute and then go right in.'

She probably hadn't meant it literally, but Maya

got her phone out to time it anyway, and saw she had a missed call from Beatrice. She felt a pang of guilt.

Beatrice and her mum knew she was in Italy but not where or why. When she'd initially told her sister her destination, Bea had immediately concluded that Maya was there in connection with the embryonic design business that had once been their joint project.

'Oh, so that supplier you were talking about, they lowered the costs, did they? That's marvellous! The samples you sent me, the colours of that wool are just perfect. The offer of the start-up money still stands, you know, it's not charity. Dante and I, we believe in you.'

The opportunity had been there for Maya to put her right, but she'd been afraid that if she started talking about Samuele and Mattio and Violetta, it would all spill out, and then the moment had passed. She had allowed the misunderstanding to go on, and the longer it had lasted the more difficult the idea of coming clean had become, and now it weighed heavily on her conscience. She would tell Bea and Mum soon, but it seemed easiest to wait until she could explain the situation in person.

Then perhaps they could explain it to me, she thought. Because when she lay awake at night wondering how she'd got herself into this situation, the answer was no more clear-cut than her feelings for Samuele were.

She was sitting with her back to him and the doorway, unaware of his presence as she slid her phone back into the big leather bag with a file sticking out that she wore slung over her shoulder.

Samuele couldn't see her face, but he'd spotted the tension in her narrow back and he found himself wondering about the person on the other end of the line who had put it there.

'Good morning, Maya.'

She got to her feet as though shot and spun around, her colour-clash statement relatively sedate today. She had on an acid-green shirt tucked into a pair of black pedal pushers, and she wore flat black pumps embellished with embroidery on her narrow feet. Her glorious hair was confined at the nape of her slender neck by a leather lace.

Samuele could almost see the boundaries that he had spent the last two weeks constructing dissolve. In his mind he was immediately unfastening the tie and spreading out her hair down her back—which in this fantasy was naked.

She was naked quite a lot in his mind. Actually, she was in his mind far too much, full stop.

'H-hello,' she stammered out. 'She said to come in but I…wasn't sure.'

He had not been sure either, but he was now.

You did not need to have second sight to see what was coming down the line. Violetta was already hinting— *taunting* might be more accurate—the fact that she felt she held the winning card. But her inability to resist turning the knife in his back had actually worked in his favour this time.

He had given himself time to stall by paying her latest thinly disguised blackmail demand, but he had no illusions that it would be the last one. And when she got bored with taking money off him, she would move in for the kill.

It was not really about money or maternal feelings for Violetta; it was all about revenge and power plays.

The money didn't matter to him, but Mattio did, and he was prepared to go to any length to fulfill his promise to his brother—including marriage.

He'd sworn to Cristiano that he would always do what was best for Mattio, and he was ashamed that he'd been willing to deprive the baby of the sort of mother he deserved just because Samuele hadn't looked beyond his own fears of becoming like his father or brother.

But he wasn't either of them, and he could see now that it had been ridiculous to compare his situation with theirs. For starters, poor Cristiano had not been able to see a single fault in his toxic bride and his deluded father's obsession had made him similarly blinkered. While *he* was perfectly aware of Maya's flaws—it was hard not to be when she was the most challenging female he had ever met!—he was certain she would make the best mother to Mattio, and the fact that there was already a blood tie between the two could be an important factor in securing her agreement to his plan.

'Do you want to come through...?'

Maya's heart flipped at the sound of his voice, but before she could respond he was already moving towards the door, taking her agreement as a given. And who could blame him? She hadn't been resisting much of late; maybe once a people-pleaser, always a people-pleaser.

Taking a deep breath, and hating the idea she might be a pushover, she clutched her bag containing the folder and followed him through to his inner sanctum.

As with three quarters of the sprawling castle, this was a room she had never entered—it was probably the first and last time.

She hadn't been sure what to expect, but it was actually pretty modern and utilitarian, dominated by a massive desk with several computer screens. One wall was book-lined, and there was a stack of free weights on a purpose-built stand. She pushed away the mental picture of a sweaty Samuele taking a break from the stress of moving around billions by stretching his muscles to the limit, and focused on the only decorative touch, which was a black and white framed drawing of the castello.

He saw her looking at it. 'The artist is disputed but it shows the place before the more contemporary additions, as in sixteenth-century contemporary.'

'It's very striking.'

He had moved to stand in front of the full-length window, and she tried hard not to sigh wistfully. He was wearing a beautifully tailored dark suit, making him looking formal, exclusive, distant and quite incredibly gorgeous.

'Th...This is a very nice room...'

He cut across her stuttering opening and nodded to one of the leather chairs set on the opposite side of the desk from him. 'Have a seat.' He took his own seat behind the massive desk, which occupied a large section of the pretty large room.

Right...so far, so formal—very formal, Maya thought uncertainly, feeling as though she had been sent to the headmaster's office, though the analogy had some major flaws.

She had never felt this sexually wound up in her school days or for that matter her adult days until the day she'd met Samuele. In her head, her life was pretty much divided into the pre- and post-Samuele days, and now his presence and the knock-on effects seemed to have altered every aspect of herself.

She kept pushing away the intense feelings he aroused in her, but they just kept pushing right back. It felt like an emotional tug of war and, as much as she might call for a referee's intervention, she had already been pulled well and truly over that red line, she thought with a despairing surge of self-realisation.

Well, it was done now; she had finally allowed herself to care enough for someone and had been rejected...and she'd survived the experience. Well, for an entire fortnight she had... She took a deep, steadying breath. See, she was still breathing so it wasn't terminal! So long as he *never* discovered that she lay in bed every night *longing* for him, she could cope.

At a distance he'd sent her nervous system into meltdown; this close to him there was no possibility she could pretend, to herself at least. But although she might have lost the ability to lie to herself, she could still fake it with the best of them in front of him.

'Would you like coffee?'

'No.' She took out the file and put it on his desk. 'I've made some notes,' she offered.

He looked at her blankly.

'The applications for the nanny,' she said, all business. 'Your message didn't say, but I assumed this was what we were going to discuss?'

'Ah, yes…I thought I might go and see Mattio later, take him for walk maybe?'

'It's Rosa's afternoon off, I'm afraid,' she said, unable to resist the dig.

Did he get it or had she been too subtle? It was hard to tell. The planes and angles of his face were designed to be inscrutable, though on anyone else she would have called the dark bands along the slashing angles of his cheekbones a blush.

'You could come too.'

'Come where?' She regarded him warily, thinking that this encounter was all as tense and awkward as she'd imagined. Maybe he was working up to some sarcastic remark about her ducking out of sight at the stables the other week?

'You like the rose gardens, I understand.'

Understand…understand from who? 'What, have you got a spy network watching my every move?' She was only half joking. 'Fine, you really don't have to ask my permission to take Mattio for a walk. Tomorrow?'

She raised a cool brow. The significance of his suit, beside the fact it made him look even more exclusive and unattainable, had not been lost on her.

'I've obviously caught you on your way to...'

It could have been just about any place; he seemed to commute to many of the world's capitals the way some people took a bus to the next town, only for him it was a private jet.

'I just got back actually.' Samuele reached for his tie, loosening the constriction at his neck. 'I'd like to know how you think Mattio is getting on. If there are any changes you think should be made...any improvements...?'

He was delaying bringing up the real reason he wanted to talk to her, and he knew it. Finding the right words was not something that he normally struggled with but, in his defence, these particular words were of the life-changing variety. 'Is there anything you need?'

'Wouldn't that be something better discussed with the new nanny? There are some very good candidates here, several with rave reviews.' She was glad, of course, she told herself fiercely, that Mattio would be in the care of someone who came highly recommended by satisfied previous parents, who knew a lot more about child development than she did. She'd always known she had been a brief stopgap in a desperate situation, but the knowledge that her time left with Mattio was coming to a swift end felt like a heavy weight pressing on her chest.

'I have...a...' He paused and dragged a hand down

his cleanly shaven cheek before clenching his long fingers into a fist. It was so unlike his normal cool, articulate self that she stared. Perhaps his thoughts were still on whatever high-powered business had taken him away from home this time.

The tension in the room was almost a physical presence; suddenly she couldn't stand it any more and surged to her feet.

'Look, shall I come back if you're…busy,' she hastily substituted, thinking *distracted* was nearer the mark.

He watched silently as she turned and moved towards the door, offering no opinion on what she'd just said… She stopped and swung back, the feelings that she had been suppressing suddenly bubbling to the surface and spilling out into hasty speech.

'Look, I *know* it was just meaningless sex and I *know* that it's not going to happen again, so treating me with simple basic *civility* is not going to raise my expectations for a repeat performance.' Her dark angry eyes raked his face. 'Are you *punishing* me for sleeping with you by ignoring me? I wasn't stalking you the other morning, you know—I was just passing by. How was I to know you were some sort of horse whisperer? Oh, God!' She finally ran out of breath but not nearly soon enough.

Her horror-filled eyes met his momentarily before she squeezed them closed, and with nothing to duck down behind this time, she covered her face with her hands instead.

She kept them there as his hands on her shoulders guided her back to the chair and then pushed her into it again.

'It was the best meaningless sex I have ever had—*you* were the best meaningless sex I have ever had.' Maybe meaningless sex was all he was capable of, Samuele thought bleakly. Not that he envied his father or his brother, but at least they had been capable of feeling a deep unselfish love for someone else, even if it had been based on lies.

Her hands fell away. 'Am I meant to be flattered—?' She broke off when she registered the expression on his face.

His eyes were filled with emotions too intense and complex for her to even begin to guess the cause and his grin lacked its normal voltage.

'I could have phrased that better,' he admitted, but that was clearly as much as he was prepared to admit.

'It's always nice to be good at something. I could put it on my next CV. Good with children and great at meaningless sex…'

He didn't smile, but then she didn't smile either; it had been a very bad joke.

The look in his eyes was really worrying her—he'd probably reject her concern, but what the hell? 'What's wrong?'

She didn't really expect a response to her blunt question, not one so unambiguous, or immediate, or sad.

'It would have been my brother's twenty-ninth birthday today.'

The last vestiges of her animosity and resentment shrivelled away and her tender heart ached with empathy for the pain etched on his face.

'Hearing people here talk about him, he sounded as if he was a good person.'

He nodded. 'He would have been a wonderful father and I think he would think you are acting like a wonderful mother—'

Was this his subtle way of saying she had overstepped her authority?

'I know I'm not Mattio's mother.'

'You're more of a mother to him than the one he's had,' he pushed out in a bitter voice. 'I've never previously thought that a mother figure was essential for a child's well-being and development, but I think I was wrong.'

'You're not going to give him back to Violetta!' she cried in horror. 'I know that legally she is his mother but—'

'No, I'm not letting him go back to Violetta,' he promised, the metallic glint in his eyes as hard as his voice.

Some of the tension left her shoulders but Maya, who had surged to her feet, stayed standing. Samuele moved around the desk and sat on the edge facing her, now at eye level, his long legs stretched out in front of him.

'And apparently, we are to expect a wedding invitation from her soon.'

'So what does that mean? Do you think that she'll try to take Mattio back?'

'I would say that's inevitable.'

'But she doesn't love him!'

'You know how convincing she can be, Maya.'

Her eyes fell as she remembered how easily her half-sister had fooled her. 'Oh, God! But this Charlie she's marrying…didn't you say he doesn't want children?' she cried, clinging to this straw of hope, not wanting to contemplate Mattio being caught up in a toxic tug of war.

'I have no doubt that before long Charlie will do anything she asks just to keep her happy. It's what Cristiano did.'

'But she'll abandon Mattio again! And this time, you might not find him.' Her face creased in anguish at the thought. 'You *can't* let her do that to him,' she declared fiercely.

'I have no intention of allowing her to do that. I intend to make a full custody claim. In the meantime I will keep paying up just to keep her quiet. It's better for now if she thinks she is winning.'

'Paying up?' Comprehension hit her. 'She is *black-mailing* you?'

He shrugged and gave a dry smile. 'Very carefully worded blackmail, but essentially yes.'

'But isn't her Charlie disgustingly rich…?'

'It's not about the money for Violetta—this is about her wreaking revenge on me for thwarting her claim to half the Agosti estate. And it's about power. Remember, she does hold a trump card, actually more than one. You said it to me yourself back at your flat, didn't you? Any court will initially favour a mother over other family members, and Mattio needs a mother in his life at least for the early years.'

She fixed him with an unwavering gaze and wondered at what age he imagined that you *stopped* needing your mother.

'The obvious solution is for me to marry.'

'So have you changed your mind about marriage?' she asked, taken aback.

'Not about marriage as an institution, no, but about being married, yes.'

'Is there a difference?'

'I think if *true love*,' he drawled contemptuously, '*really* existed, then marriage would be redundant. Two people wouldn't need a legal framework to trap them together.'

'Trap…?'

'Oh, I know divorce is relatively simple nowadays, but so many hang on in there when it's obvious it's beyond hope of saving. Marriage is just a contract, not some sort of magical spell that grants eternal happiness and joy. If it's drawn up with both parties' interests in mind, the duration of the contract is flexible and there are no unreasonable expectations like monogamy, then I see no reason why it couldn't be successful.'

'Successful maybe, but it's not really marriage, is it?' This cold-blooded description horrified her.

'An open marriage.'

'So not really marriage at all, then! Because marriage is about faith, trust...' She couldn't bring herself to say *love* or even think the word while she was in the same room as Samuele.

'Marriage in this case is about securing the future security and happiness of my brother's child.'

'Of course, but—' Her thoughts skidded to an abrupt stop and she had to try and conceal a gasp of shock. She had been hanging onto a rock wall of denial by her fingernails for weeks and she'd finally lost her grip.

Not being able to say the word in a man's presence wasn't exactly one of the most recognised symptoms of being in love, but, nevertheless, she was.

She had fallen in love with a man who was capable of giving his love and loyalty to a child that carried the bloodline he was so proud of, and to the land that was his heritage. A man who thought marriage *might* work, but only if you took love out of the equation. There was no room in his life for a woman, no room for her.

She wasn't sure if it was a bitter laugh or a despairing sob that was locked in her throat, but it hurt as she remembered that she'd always believed *not* falling in love with the wrong man was a matter of choice. She marvelled now at her own arrogance and was suddenly deeply fearful for her future.

'So you see that I didn't ask you here to talk about nannies, because I am very much hoping that there will be no need for one.'

She had started shaking her head. 'You want me to stay on here until you've found a suitable wife?'

'I want you to stay on here—but as my wife.'

He watched her drop down into the chair she had recently vacated. Luckily it was still there, though he doubted she would have noticed if she'd landed on the floor.

'That is *insane*!' Her laugh was edged with hysteria. 'The only thing we have in common is Mattio.'

'Isn't that enough?' His shoulders lifted as his dark eyes moved over her face, lingering on the plump curve of her lips. 'But actually it's not true. We also have a similar sexual appetite, don't we? What we have, between us—that kind of chemistry is rare, *cara*, and exceptional sex is even rarer.' Two years of enjoying the pleasures of Maya's body and exhausting his hunger for her would surely compensate for any temporary loss of freedom.

Breathing hard by the time he finished speaking, Maya shook her head in an effort to free her mind from the spell of his smoky voice and the erotic images his words had evoked.

'Yes, we *do* have Mattio.' His delivery was now flat and cool. 'And he deserves the very best. You are the best for him, and there is the blood connection between you, which, given the circumstances, could be a significant factor.' He paused, his crazily long lashes veiling his eyes momentarily.

'I know he's the last bit of your brother you have left and the heir to—'

'He is the heir to the Agosti name,' Samuele cut in. 'And the responsibility that goes with it. But he is not Cristiano's child.'

The blood left her face and her heart went into high gear. She could hardly hear past the dull thud in her own chest; whatever she had expected to hear, this was definitely not it. 'What are you saying?' she whispered, her eyes trained on his face.

'That, unlike you, I have no blood connection with Mattio,' he said roughly, in a voice that cracked with the effort to keep it free of emotion.

'This is the thing that Violetta is blackmailing you about.'

He shrugged. 'It's her trump card.'

'How long have you known?'

'Cristiano told me before he died, when he asked me to keep Mattio safe, to take care of him.'

'Your brother knew that the baby wasn't his?' Her thoughts raced to process the flow of information.

'Violetta couldn't hide it—the dates made it utterly impossible. Cristiano told me he was out of the country for a significant amount of time when Mattio was conceived. If my brother had lived he would have been the child's father and that is all that mattered to him…'

Would he have been as big a man as his brother? It was a question Samuele had asked himself many times. How could any man know the answer until he was faced with the situation himself?

'Mattio *is* an Agosti, he *is* my heir and I will do

anything it takes to keep him safe and keep my promise to my brother.'

Including marrying me.

'Who else knows about this?' she asked.

'I have told no one but you.'

His trust and giving her joint responsibility for the secret he had shared with her changed things in a way she could not put words to—it altered the dynamic between them.

Samuele trained his gaze on her face. 'I'm asking for two years of your life… You would still be young enough later to go on and have a family of your own,' he pointed out, conscious of an odd ache in his chest at the thought of her holding children she'd created with another man. 'There would, of course, be the option to extend that period should both parties be agreeable, and the golden handshake you'll receive at the termination of the marriage would obviously mean that you'd be able to maintain the living standards you'd have become accustomed to.'

'I don't give a damn about money!' she snapped. She wanted his love and he was offering her a soulless marriage.

He watched as she covered her face with her hands again and felt a tug of guilt.

'We have nothing in common… Look at this place,' she said, spreading her hands wide to encompass the room and everything beyond.

'We do. We both love Mattio.'

The response cut right through her defences and

directly into her weakness. *Love...* She did love Mattio, but she loved Samuele too. Only what the heart wants the heart can't always have... *But isn't it better to enjoy what the heart can have while it lasts?* that insidious voice tempted.

Halfway through the internal dialogue she realised that she was actually considering it. Maybe he read the self-revelation on her face because he put his hand in his pocket and pulled out a small box.

He opened the box, flicking the catch up with his finger to reveal a velvet lining that was old and worn. Maya wasn't looking at the box, but the prize it contained, a prize that would be a great big fat lie on her finger.

'This was my grandmother's, with a few greats added, who was Russian originally. I repurchased it quite recently.' Along with several other items with a similar Russian royal family provenance. He could already see in his mind's eye the emerald necklace in the stunning enamelled setting sitting comfortably between Maya's lovely breasts... The image came with a distracting rush of that mix of painful yet pleasurable heat.

With a tiny gasp she put her hand to her mouth, her big eyes going from the ring to his face and back again. Even he could see that the square-cut emerald surrounded with clusters of brilliant diamonds, set on a wide gold band etched with a scroll pattern and inlaid with yet more precious stones, was stunningly beautiful.

She shook her head.

'People often marry because there is a baby,' he pressed. 'The baby might not be ours, but is this situation so very different? The principle is the same, securing the welfare of a vulnerable child.'

Maya looked up at him, loving every line, every carved angle and patrician hollow of his face... She also loved Mattio and she knew her heart would break if she left him. She had so much love to give, so wasn't it genuinely better to give it even knowing that, in this case, it would never be returned?

It was as if all her secret dreams of love and her worst nightmares about abandonment had collided. She couldn't possibly see how this would end well for her, but Samuele was right about one thing: Mattio had to be protected.

Her hand shook as he slid the ring on her finger. It was a perfect fit.

'I have one stipulation. *I* don't think that monogamy is an unrealistic expectation.' She could stand many things, but that was the one betrayal that she knew would totally crush her.

There was a pause, then he said slowly, 'I think I can accommodate that.'

She immediately started tugging the ring off her finger. 'What are you doing?' he asked sharply.

'Taking it off. I can't walk round with a fortune on

my finger. We can wait until things are official and I've told my family.' *Oh, God, my family!* she groaned inside.

'Things are already official, so I see no reason to wait. It is the formal opening of the Villa Agosti gallery in Florence in two weeks, so your first official role as my bride-to-be will be to act as hostess.'

'I'm not really a front-of-house sort of girl, Samuele. I am more backstage, prop moving, that sort of thing. I thought I'd just be doing nursery things.'

'You will be doing all the things that would be expected of my fiancée,' he said flatly.

The emphasis on *all* made her sensitive tummy muscles quiver. 'What,' she asked, her alarm shifting up a gear as he framed her face with his hands, 'are you doing?' Silly question—it was pretty obvious what he was doing.

The kiss was long and hard and depleted her of any final remnants of resistance. 'I am making it official,' he rasped throatily, before picking her up and sitting her on the desk, then slowly pushing her back until she lay there watching through half-closed eyes as he threw his tie across the room.

'What if someone comes in?' As resistance went it was pretty half-hearted.

'If you even notice, *cara*, I will be deeply insulted.'

Her breath quickened. 'You make a lot of assumptions…'

He gave a wolfish grin, oozing arrogance from every perfect pore as he planted a hand flat on the wooden surface either side of her face. 'I don't think it is an *assumption*—' she whimpered low in her throat as his scorching lips moved up the column of her neck '—to say that we definitely do not need a rule book in our bedroom.'

CHAPTER TEN

MAYA SMILED, AND a low husky laugh vibrated in her throat as her fingers tangled in the dark hair of the man whose head lay nestled between her breasts in the bed she had shared with him for the last two weeks.

'What are you laughing at?'

'You… No, not really,' she added quickly. It was just she had never imagined that sex could involve humour.

The depth of the sharp soul-piercing tenderness she felt for Samuele was something she had never dreamt of either. As for the desperate raw passion he could awaken in her, she sometimes didn't even recognise herself in the woman she became in his arms.

His head lifted, his dark heavy-lidded eyes still slumbrous from their recent lovemaking.

'I just remembered you saying we didn't need a rule book in the bedroom.' She gave a languid sigh as he slid his way up her body until their faces were level.

'I remember that too.'

Samuele could count on one hand the times he had spent more than one night with the same woman, be-

cause the next night would have been much the same
and, put quite simply, he had a low boredom threshold.

He had heard it suggested that he was attracted by
the thrill of the hunt but in reality there rarely had
been a hunt. He didn't make the mistake of putting
that down to his own irresistibility; he believed women
were attracted by what he represented to them, which
was money, power and his supposedly glamorous lifestyle.

He looked at the lovely face inches from his own,
no make-up, hair wild, flushed cheeks. No two nights
were the same with Maya; her glorious lack of inhibi-
tion, her innate sensuality and the fact she gave everything of herself every single time they made love made
her the sexiest woman he could ever have imagined.

He quite simply could not get enough of her. His
idea of heaven was being stranded on a desert island
and having her five times a day, but even that wouldn't
be enough; where Maya was concerned, he'd discovered he was insatiable.

'You taste of me,' he said, dipping his tongue into
the warmth of her mouth.

'You taste so good too,' she husked against his lips,
meeting his tongue with her own.

Sometimes during moments like this Maya could
hardly believe the level of intimacy between them, and
how natural, how *right* it all felt.

'I should get up,' she said, not moving.

'You're still worried about tonight?'

Samuele felt a by now familiar surge of tenderness

as she grimaced and gave a little shrug. Maya never went for the sympathy vote.

'Don't be, *cara*,' he said, pulling himself into a sitting position and dragging a hand through his tousled hair.

'Easy for you to say—you're used to being stared at.' *And lusted after,* she added silently as her eyes followed the liquid glide of perfectly formed muscles under golden skin as he stretched hugely.

'And you're not?' There was a lack of vanity and then there was blindness. 'You must know that you are an incredibly beautiful woman and you certainly don't dress to be invisible.' He sensed her stiffening and tagged on quickly, 'Which is good—I really like your sense of style.'

'I don't want my self-worth to be based on the way I look, Samuele, because looks fade.'

'I think you have a few years left yet,' he teased, taking pleasure just from studying the delicate lines of her face. It was young and smooth now but, gifted with a bone structure like hers, experience and time would only enhance what she had.

She flashed him a quick glance from under her lashes before looking away and muttering, 'I was invisible once.'

His fingers, moving in a sensual sweep down her spine, stilled. 'Your stepfather?'

Astonished eyes flew to his face. 'How on earth did you know it was him?'

'A couple of things you've said.'

And he'd remembered? *Do not go there, Maya, do not start seeing what you want to see.* He's observant, that's all. A skill that had helped make him a respected name in the world of finance. Her Internet research had revealed that about him, also that the respect came tinged with a healthy dose of fear; he had a reputation for total ruthlessness.

He was certainly a ruthlessly efficient lover.

'Edward seemed nice, kind, caring before they were married, but afterwards he changed, at least when Mum wasn't around, towards me and Beatrice. I was so afraid of him—'

Beside her she could feel Samuele stiffen, and he swore and said something harsh in his mother tongue.

'No…no…' she said, laying a pacific hand against his heaving chest. 'There was nothing physical and it was only little things at first. Everything I did he mocked, like a birthday card I made for Mum once. He looked at it and laughed and threw it in the bin saying that I couldn't give her that sort of rubbish.'

Samuele's big strong hand came to cover hers, his fingers sliding in between hers. She smiled her gratitude; the warm pressure was comforting.

'He chipped away at my self-esteem until in the end I didn't have any, no confidence at all. He used to say the only thing I had going for me was a pretty face and when I started getting teenage acne he had an absolute field day!' She felt Samuele's fingers tighten around her own. 'I would dread him coming in and finding something about me to laugh at. I wanted so badly to be invisible and I eventually became a grey little mouse scared of her own shadow.

'I don't know what would have happened if it wasn't for Beatrice. She was tougher than me, and she gave as good as she got, so he didn't pick on her as much. Mum had it bad too. He wanted a child that was *his* child, and she went through cycle after cycle of IVF to try and please him. It affected her health terribly but he acted as if he was the injured party.

'Maybe that was when she started to see what he really was, and she began actually listening to what Bea and I told her, and believing us. I will always remember the expression on his face when he arrived home and she'd packed his bags.

'I saw a therapist.' She glanced at him to see how he took this. There were still some very outdated views out there about mental health.

'That's really good,' Samuele said, struggling to keep the burning anger that was consuming him from his voice at the picture she'd painted that he knew only hinted at the true extent of all she had suffered. The need to reach out and comfort her was alien to him and he wasn't quite sure what to do. 'Did it help?'

'It did help, yes, but Mum still tries to compensate. She feels guilty that she didn't see what he was doing. I hate that she and Bea still feel like that, as though I'm weak or fragile and they have to protect me.'

'So you became the unbreakable Maya Monk.' In her bold, bright colours and her hit-the-world-head-on attitude. But underneath all that armour, she was the little girl who had been the victim of a coercive, controlling bully.

She was, he decided, the strongest person he had ever met.

Maya blinked, realising with a sense of shock just how much she had told him, more than she had ever admitted outside the therapist's office, probably more than she had admitted inside it too!

'I suppose I should get up,' she said, suddenly feeling shy and exposed...although *exposed* was a funny word to use when he had seen every little bit of her, loved every little bit of her.

It was moments like this, when everything felt perfect, that she often heard Edward's voice telling her she wasn't good enough, that she didn't deserve to be loved by anyone.

She listened and there was nothing.

She rolled back to Samuele and took his face between her hands. 'Thank you!' she said fiercely.

'For what?'

You made me believe that I'm worth loving.

There was a quizzical furrow in his brow as he studied her face and tried to interpret her silence. 'The gallery opening will be hard for you, won't it?'

'I'll be fine.'

He recognised her factory-setting response for what it was—a cover for the fact that she was not all right at all. He felt guilty for the times he had taken it at face value because it had suited him to do so.

'You'll be fine, I know, and I'll be there for you tonight. You won't be alone because I will be with you every step of the way. Oh, and if you *really* want to say thank you, I can think of several ways...'

She gave a sultry smile. 'So can I.'

'I haven't seen anyone older than nine years old literally press their nose to the window like that before.'

She sniffed and rubbed the fading mist from the window before settling back into her seat. 'I'm sure it's very *uncool* to be excited, but you know what?'

'You don't care,' he completed seamlessly.

'Not even a little bit. Florence may be your backyard but to me it's...' She mimicked one of his shrugs when words failed her.

'I don't take it for granted, though. Actually I *like* seeing the world through your eyes, though only occasionally. Otherwise I'd have given away all my possessions by now to a charity for donkeys.'

'It was a worthy cause and you shouldn't have been looking at my bank statement!'

'You left your laptop open on my desk.'

She gave a little snort and looked out of the window again. They had left the river and the cathedral behind when the car in front slowed. As they approached a building with a classical facade set back from the road behind an elaborate wall, Mattio stirred slightly, his sleepy brown eyes opening briefly before they closed again. They took a sharp right and drove through the archway into the private internal courtyard, and Maya straightened in her seat, bracing herself for the inevitable meet and greet.

'You'll be fine, *cara*, you have nothing to prove.'

Only she did, and he had to know it. He couldn't be that naive, could he? She was about to marry Samuele Agosti, not only the most handsome man on the planet, but also a legend in his own lifetime. The interest in their engagement wasn't just trending on social media, there were several column inches devoted to the upcoming marriage in all the serious financial journals.

She tried to focus on the pluses, which included the fact that Beatrice wouldn't be here tonight. She loved her sister dearly, but not the awkward questions she would inevitably ask.

Poor Beatrice's morning sickness had got worse, necessitating bed rest and an intravenous drip, so she had been admitted to hospital for a while. Back home now, she was being fiercely guarded by Dante and their mum.

Maya's mother was set to meet Samuele next week when she would fly out to spend a couple of weeks at the castello.

So all she had to do tonight was cope with the world's press, half of whom seemed to want to know up front *who* she would be wearing tonight.

The only thing that was stopping her running for the hills was the security of knowing that Samuele would be at her side. His support made all the difference to her.

As she slid out of the air-conditioned car into the

fragrant afternoon warmth she knew her mind should have been on higher things than wondering which of the outfits she had brought with her to wear tonight. But first impressions counted, and photos that were taken tonight would be images the whole world would look at tomorrow and in the days and weeks to come.

Also her choice of dress was one of the few things she felt she had some control over. She tucked her finger, weighted down by the beautiful heirloom ring, into her pocket and emptied her mind of worries. She was determined to take pleasure from the beauty of the cloistered space with the rows of fountains, their spray catching and reflecting the light as it fell into a long central pool.

As she tilted her head to examine the seemingly endless number of windows that looked down from the wrought-iron balconies on three sides of the space, the sun dazzled her and made her blink as she brushed stray strands of hair off her face.

'Good journey?'

Maya smiled as she identified the familiar lanky figure of Samuele's male private secretary, Diego, a nice, friendly reception committee of one. A combination of his youth and his ready smile made Diego, who had travelled ahead with all the bags and baggage—one small child and a white tie event meant they were not travelling light—someone she could relax around.

'And you?'

'Fine—' His glance drifted to where Samuele stood, a phone pressed to his ear, a daunting frown pleating his brow visible for a moment before he turned, presenting his broad shoulders to them.

Maya tried not to register the obvious tension in his back and widened her smile to include Rosa, who had stayed the night with relatives in the city and volunteered to help out tonight. 'Hi, Rosa, I hope your family are well.' She glanced towards the open door of the car and the sleeping child. 'He slept all the way here. I probably should have woken him but he looked so peaceful.'

On cue Mattio opened his eyes and started squirming in his seat. Maya moved to unclip his belt but Rosa, neat in a practical pair of chinos and blue shirt, beat her to it. 'I've already scoped out the nursery. Shall I give him his feed?'

'Would you?'

Rosa opened the stroller that had been unloaded with a practised flick of her wrist. 'We'll be in the nursery when you're ready,' she said as she snapped open the safety harness, ignoring the wail of protest from her passenger.

Maya, who saw that Samuele had finally pocketed his phone, pressed a kiss to the top of the increasingly tetchy child's head. She felt secure in the knowledge that he was safe with Rosa. She was so good with him, to the point when there were times she made Maya feel like an amateur.

Maya began to weave her way through the fountains towards the spot where Samuele stood, conscious as she did so that Diego had hung back discreetly.

As she got closer she sensed a tension in Samuele's stance, but also an excitement, which made sense. Tonight was important for Samuele, she knew that, it was the culmination of the years of rebuilding the lost family heritage that meant so much to him, not just to preserve it, but to make it relevant to the twenty-first century. Could it be that despite his seemingly laid-back attitude he was more worried about tonight than he'd let on?

'Good news, they have finally located the missing Agosti statues.'

'Oh, that's terrific!' She knew how much this news meant to Samuele, in a symbolic, end-of-the-journey sort of way.

Locating and acquiring the entire Agosti collection had been the singular most difficult element of his self-imposed task and one that many doubted was achievable.

Officially tonight was all about the Agosti collection, the largest number of ancient Roman and Greek statues in private hands in the world, now housed in the newly restored Villa Agosti, and to finally be shared with the world.

The fact that there were only half a dozen missing pieces was considered a miracle by many, but for Samuele, who did not cut himself any slack, it had constituted a failure.

'The thing is I have to go right now, because there's a Russian collector after them too…'

She pulled in a tense breath and brought her lashes

down in a self-protective sweep. 'Now? But…couldn't you send Diego? Why do you have to go in person?'

Impatient to be gone, Samuele shook his head. 'I'll be back in plenty of time before it starts tonight,' he soothed. 'It's an hour there and an hour back tops. The vendor is a pretty eccentric character, who doesn't seem so much interested in an advantageous offer as she does my star sign. She insists on meeting me in person, something to do with a *planet alignment*…?'

Maya swallowed, struggling to inject a suitably amused note into her response and failing miserably.

'She sounds pretty *interesting*. Obviously you must… It's fine, I understand. Obviously you must go,' she said. But as she spoke she was aware that her response implied he was asking her permission; the fact was he was going whether she liked it or not.

'So you're fine with this?'

She could see from the look in his eyes that he was already not here—*she* wasn't here. She clamped her teeth over the words he wanted to hear and flung out a cold and resentful response instead. 'And if I'm not would it make any difference to you?'

His lips tightened with annoyance and he sighed. 'You're making this into a big thing and it really isn't. I'll be back before you know it, certainly in time for the speech-giving later on. Diego will look after you. I'm sure I'll even make it back for the photoshoot. They want some footage of us in the gallery. Look, here's Diego now.'

The young man punched the air in triumph when Samuele outlined the developments.

'Sure…sure…' he said when Samuele told him the plan. 'Anything,' he said, turning to Maya. 'And I'm your man.'

No, she wanted to say, *you're not my man…and my man isn't really my man.* Letting herself believe otherwise was the road to madness. She was probably going to have a lot of moments like this one, so she'd better get used to it.

Moments filled with suppressed resentment. Moments when she felt very alone.

'So it's all good, then?' Samuele said distractedly.

Without replying she turned with a brilliantly insincere smile to Diego so that she wouldn't have to watch Samuele turn and walk away from her. Which of course he did.

After a prompt from her Diego was only too happy to launch into an explanation of what a feat the restoration of the villa had been.

'Restoration is a delicate balancing act, too much and you lose the authenticity. I can never get over the fact that standing here you're literally yards from the most famous historic sights of Florence.'

Maya walked alongside him as he displayed his knowledge, only hearing one word in three. She knew that the restoration of the collection was important to Samuele so she had hidden the extent of her nerves about tonight.

They kicked in hard now.

CHAPTER ELEVEN

There was no *us* involved in the gallery photoshoot. Just Maya, dwarfed, despite the high heels, by the pale statues around her, a flash of colour in a monochrome backdrop in the cerise silk shirt dress that was one of the new additions to her wardrobe, as were the dramatic thirties-style drop earrings.

To complete her transformation into a sophisticated stranger her hair had been tamed, with the help of Rosa, into a smooth ponytail. Perhaps sensing the importance of the occasion every curl stayed in dutiful submission during the mercifully short photoshoot.

Back in their private suite on the top floor of the villa, Maya reviewed her performance. While she had not said anything witty or wildly interesting, settling instead for polite, she had not said anything too stupid either, and she had neatly sidestepped the couple of questions that were invitations into controversial subjects.

Diego had said that Samuele would be proud of her.

She had wanted to retort that she didn't want his pride, she required his presence.

He had promised her he'd be there, and he had let her down. She didn't even rate a call or text to say he was running late.

'Any luck?' Maya stood up, the tulle layers of the dress she'd changed into for the speech-giving flaring around her as Rosa returned to the room.

The girl shook her head. 'No, I'm sorry, Diego can't get through to him either...it keeps going to voicemail.'

Maya compressed her lips. Five minutes ago the news had come that everyone had arrived and, with it, the gentle suggestion that it was not done to keep royalty waiting was left hanging in the air. She had felt a clenched fingernail away from total panic.

Fortunately, her mood had moved on. She no longer felt like hiding in a cupboard, she felt like hitting someone—all right, not someone, just the one person who had let her down, abandoned her to her fate, after he had *promised* to be there with her.

Just as her dad had promised he'd be back to watch her in the Christmas nativity play, but he hadn't come back, had he? They'd told her that he wouldn't be coming back, ever, but she had refused to believe them. She'd sat on the window seat looking down into the street, sure that his car would appear, totally sure because he had promised... Finally she'd fallen asleep and someone had put her to bed.

She'd waited the next day and the next but he'd never come.

She'd never forgotten the feeling, and all her life she'd been guided by a determination never to experience it again, until Samuele!

Even as she embraced her anger she knew it would eventually ebb and she'd just be left alone again.

There was a tentative tap on the door and the person who appeared in response to her *come in* revealed breathlessly, 'The royal party has arrived.'

'I'll be right there.' She knew etiquette meant she as hostess should have been there to greet them…but, thanks to her experience on San Macizo, ironically royalty was one of the few things that didn't spook her about tonight. The same could not be said for everything else.

'Right then, Rosa, he's a no-show so let's do this.' She glanced at herself in the mirror, and decided she looked like a cross between an old-fashioned Southern belle and a lampshade. 'But no, not in this meringue of a dress. Help me out of it, will you, Rosa?'

A wide-eyed Rosa obliged, helping Maya to slip into her second choice for tonight, which had actually been her first choice before she'd doubted herself.

Five minutes later she looked at her reflection in the same mirror and a very different Maya looked back, a much more edgy, sexy Maya.

The pretty froth of pale lemon tulle was gone, and in its place was a scarlet full-length silk slip dress; simple and dramatic, it clung lovingly to the curves of her body.

She had added a dash of old red lipstick on top of the frosted gloss she had previously applied and it didn't take much to intensify the grey eyeshadow she wore to give it a smoky effect.

If she'd had time she would have put her hair down again, but while she had pretended an indifference to the waiting royalty, she was aware that she really didn't have time to hang around, so her hair would have to stay in the classic chignon that it had been tamed into, emphasising the length of her slender neck.

She stood poised at the top of the stairs underneath the spotlight of a chandelier, conscious of a sea of eyes looking up at her, her heart thudding frantically. There was a split second when she wanted to pick up her skirts and run away as fast as she could.

Then she focused on one face, she had no idea who it was, but blanking out the rest worked. She got down the stairs, and the rest was a blur. She parried the obvious questions about Samuele's absence without actually giving a straight answer, but luckily most people didn't seem to realise it until she had moved on.

Every lie and prevarication had only built the resentful head of steam that was choking her. Perhaps he was making a blatant point that her importance in his life came way below a bunch of statues?

Her homework on the collection paid off; she was able to give intelligent responses to several questions. There were a few speeches, people said complimen-

tary things about the evening and her…and then she
was told it was her turn.

'What?' she whispered frantically to Diego, who
had pretty much been her shadow all evening.

'Well, officially it is—'

'Samuele's turn,' she bit out.

Diego gave her an understanding look. 'There is
no need for you to do it. I could make a small speech
apologising—'

She was tempted—oh, my, but she was *so* tempted
to let him do that—but she shook her head. 'No, that's
fine, I can do this.'

'I'll introduce you, shall I?'

'That would be good, thank you, Diego.'

She actually had no idea in the world what she was
going to say until she started.

'I'm sure you're all wondering where Samuele is—
well, so am I!'

She paused for the ripple of laughter, which came
satisfyingly on cue. Sometimes the truth worked better than a lie. Samuele didn't ever explain himself to
anyone, so why should she do so in his absence?

'The fact we are here tonight is a testament to one
man's determination and single-minded vision, not to
preserve this collection, but to celebrate it. Because
the past is an organic living thing, which has shaped
all our presents and our futures…'

She sensed Diego, who up until that point had
looked ready to stage a face-saving intervention, relax.
And she continued to speak.

* * *

The adrenaline was already fading before she reached the privacy of her room, having checked on Mattio and been assured by Rosa, who had an adjoining room to the nursery, that she would get up in the night if needed.

By the time Maya had closed the door it had gone completely. She could barely stand and she was shaking with anger.

She looked at the champagne in the silver bucket, the two glasses clearly ordered earlier before Samuele had got a better offer. Presumably he was somewhere celebrating his latest acquisition with someone else. A female someone else.

She walked across and picked up the bottle.

During the evening she had imagined, numerous times, the pleasure of throwing his ring in his face and walking away.

But the moment she had looked at the sleeping baby she'd known that was not an option open to her. The trouble was she'd made the mistake of equating great sex with caring, possibly even love. She shook her head at the extent of her own wilful stupidity.

She had allowed herself to believe that Samuele had started to care for her, that his tenderness in the bedroom and the closeness they enjoyed there had translated to them as a couple outside the bedroom too.

Well, tonight her self-deception had been revealed in all its horrific glory, and she only had herself to blame. She was convenient in bed; outside it, she was only there for Mattio. In fact, she was little more than a nanny with a ring.

Samuele fought his instinct to go straight to his room, but fortunately he almost immediately bumped into Diego.

The other man's jaw dropped in shock. 'What happened to you?'

Samuele dragged a hand across his hair to remove some of the excess moisture. 'I fell into a river. Could you get me some dry clothes? I'll get changed before I—'

'Of course, of course…did you get the statues?'

'Never actually got there,' Samuele admitted, not adding that he'd got halfway there and turned back. With every mile he had driven the image of the expression on Maya's face that had said she was far from fine hadn't faded; it had got clearer, as had the excuses he had used to assuage his guilt.

Yes, the acquisition of those statues would finally give him closure over what his father had done, but at what cost? People broke promises every day, and yet he'd convinced himself he would be back in time, and that, even if he wasn't, it would be good for Maya to face her fears.

Like you're facing yours, had mocked his inner critic as the small pokes attacking his conscience had become a sharp knife blade.

Cursing, he had taken the return exit at the last moment and, ignoring the recalculations of the onboard satnav, he'd headed back to the city.

He'd almost made it too. He would have done, if he hadn't glanced across at the exact moment that guy had climbed onto the railings of the bridge.

By the time he'd reached the foot of the bridge there had been quite an audience gathered. Several had been taking videos on their phones yet no one had been going near him.

'Has someone called the police?'

'An ambulance more like…'

'Yes, I called them—and an ambulance.'

There was a communal gasp as the man tottered.

Samuele swore and began to climb the bank towards the pedestrian path across the bridge.

'Keep back!' the guy yelled hoarsely.

Hell, he looked so young! What could lead someone with their whole life ahead of them to a place like this? 'Fine, I'm not coming nearer to you, but I'm afraid I can't hear very well, so I'm just going to climb a bit higher.' He put a hand up and vaulted onto the guard rail where the man stood, though still a good twenty feet away.

'I'm not going to come any closer… My name is Samuele…and yours is…?'

'Go away! I know what you're trying to do!'

Which is more, Samuele thought wryly, *than I do.* It wasn't really a matter of doing the right thing; it was more a matter of doing something. Something that hopefully didn't make a bad situation even worse...

The thing was, he really thought that he was talking the man down, or at the very least injecting some level of calm into the situation, but it was the sound of a police siren that did it. One moment he was listening to Samuele tell him that he too had lost someone he loved very much and the next he had just launched himself off the bridge into the river below.

Samuele's response had been less down to finely honed logic and more to a split-second instinct. He'd jumped in after him.

'Sorry I left you in the lurch like that. Did you have my notes for the speech?' he asked Diego, stripping off his wet shirt and fighting his way into the clean one that had been provided.

'I did. But actually, your fiancée, she gave the whole speech herself.'

In the act of zipping himself into dry trousers Samuele froze and ground out a curse.

'Actually she—'

Samuele silenced him with a hand. 'No, it's all right.' Although it really wasn't. 'It's not your fault. I'll get this—'

'But—'

'It's fine, Diego, leave it to me.'

Maya had kicked off her shoes but she was still wearing the red dress and she was still raging high on her second wind of fatigue-defying fury when the door opened.

She knew exactly who was standing there but she didn't turn her head as she crammed the last item into the case and forced the lid closed before she straightened up.

'I am so, so sorry, *cara*.'

'Oh, well, then, that makes everything all right, doesn't it?'

She moved towards him with a sexy glide of red silk that sent a surge of heat through Samuele's body. 'I'm sure,' he rasped, 'that it's not as bad as you think. I'll phone around and do a bit of damage control.' He took in the significance of the cases and his expression altered, his eyes hardening. 'You're not going anywhere.'

'No, I'm not—you are.'

'What?'

'Don't look so worried, it's not as if you'll have to resort to sofa surfing, but the thing is I just didn't want to sleep in the same room as you!'

'*Dio*, Maya, I know it must have been bad tonight but—'

'You think I made a fool of myself, don't you?' she said. 'Well, it's always good to know what a wonderful opinion you have of me, but sorry, I don't require your efforts in damage limitation, because I smashed it—I was a success, brilliant.'

'That's fantastic! I knew you could do it—'

She folded her arms across her heaving chest and directed a narrow-eyed glare up at his face. 'Not two minutes ago, you didn't! You thought I'd fall flat on my face and you let me do it because you're a selfish bastard who really doesn't give a damn about me.'

'Look, I'm sorry but tonight—I shouldn't have left in the first place. I should have refused to jump through hoops for the sake of the statues.'

'Easy to be wise in hindsight,' she sneered. 'Tonight you did me a favour—it really brought a few thing into focus. I would walk away from you right now if it weren't for Mattio, but *he* needs me, so *I* won't abandon him. I will marry you, and I will do this sort of nonsense tonight, but I will *not* continue to share my bed with a man who cares more about a few lumps of old marble than he does about keeping p…promises he has m…made to people.' She scrunched her eyes closed and stood there, her hands clenched into fists. 'I will not cry over you.'

'Oh, *cara*…'

Her eyes flew open again, wide, dark and stormy. 'Don't *"cara"* me! I am making the rules now. I was a very good deal for you, Samuele, and you blew it!'

'My God, you're so gorgeous.' With a hunger approaching desperation, his eyes moved over the soft, delicate contours of her face.

'Do you really think that a few compliments will make me melt into your arms? Oh, yes,' she added, in full flow now, 'and I have decided I want to alter the terms of our *contract*. That open-marriage deal you suggested? I've started to think it's a damned great idea!'

It took a while for his brain to decipher the words she'd just spoken, but when it did he went pale and literally swayed where he stood.

'Open marriage?' His woman seeing another man? *His* Maya, his *wife*, being touched, made love to by someone else? The reaction to the images in his head rippled through him like an electrical charge and his body went rigid with rejection. He scowled fiercely. 'I don't think so.'

A sudden need to reach out to her made him take a step forward but then she snapped out, 'It was your idea to begin with, *remember*? And unlike most of your ideas, I think it's a good one. Very *civilised*!' she hissed.

'This is all just a misunderstanding,' he protested.

'No, it's not. Have you even heard a word I've said? I hate you!'

'Let me explain…' He stopped as his voice was drowned out by a loud wail.

'Now look what you've done!' she accused, pushing open the door into the living room that separated the bedroom from the nursery wing.

Samuele, a step behind her, stopped short when they entered the nursery, where the wail was now almost deafening. Rosa was standing there with the crying baby in her arms.

She gave Maya a look of gratitude as the baby was transferred to her.

Samuele heaved a sigh of frustration. 'We'll speak again in the morning.'

* * *

The first thing Maya did the next morning, after she had applied the cold compresses to her eyes to help the puffiness that was the cost of crying herself to sleep, was scroll down her phone to see if she had been as much of a success as she had boasted to Samuele.

She typed in the word Agosti and waited for the results. The news of the gala was there but preceding it was the headline: *Italian Banker in Dramatic River Rescue!*

She swung her legs over the side of the bed and clicked the viral video attached to the headline.

The video was still playing when she ran into the sitting room where Samuele was sitting on one of the sofas, looking as though he hadn't slept a wink.

She looked wildly from the phone in her hand to him. 'Why didn't you tell me?'

'I was waiting for you to wake up.'

'You jumped off a bridge!' She was shaking the phone at him, the video still playing.

'There weren't many other options, *cara.*'

'Maybe *not* jumping off a bridge?' Her brain had been frozen with panic, but as it started working she felt dizzy with fright. *She could have lost him!* 'That's why you didn't arrive back on time, isn't it?' When she thought of all the things she'd said to him, she could have wept if she'd had any more tears left inside her. 'Why didn't you send me a message?'

'My phone was at the bottom of a river and it took

me some time to convince the hospital staff that I wasn't suicidal myself.'

'Did he…the man…did he…?'

'The jumper survived.' One day he might be grateful he was alive, but not last night—a fact he'd managed to communicate to Samuele as he had dragged him onto the shore before collapsing himself.

The things she'd said last night, the emotions she'd revealed, would be impossible to backpedal from. The only real option that Maya could see going forward was to explain that she'd reacted that way because she was so very much in love with him. In fact, she thought almost numbly, it would be a kind of relief to have it out in the open at last.

It would also be the kiss of death to any sort of ongoing relationship other than as Mattio's parents. But that wouldn't change anything either, just speed up the inevitable, because there was no way she could hide her true feelings for him for very much longer anyway. It wasn't in her nature.

He had moved to stand beside her and she could already feel her resolve slipping as the warmth of him, the well-known scent of his body, reached out and enveloped her. She clenched her hands to hide the fact she was shaking and studied her bare feet.

'Were you on your way to get the statues or…?' She despised herself for delaying the moment of truth.

'I was on my way back, but I never actually got there,' he admitted huskily.

She looked up to see that he was right there and

looking into his dark eyes made her tremble. 'I don't understand,' she whispered.

'I didn't get there because I thought you needed me. As it turned out I was wrong, and you were right—you did smash it. I am so proud of you.' He took her face between his hands. 'I am such a fool, *cara*. Even as I was turning the car around to come back to you, I wouldn't admit to myself why. I was too weak, too scared to admit that I loved you with all my heart.

'Last night when you said you wanted an open marriage I was devastated. After you sent me away I could see my whole empty *safe* life stretching out in front of me without you, and all of the things I worked so hard for, they would mean nothing if you are not in my life, by my side. I know that you wear my ring already, *cara*, but I never asked you to marry me, not really. So, Maya, will you please be my wife and I promise I will try every day of our lives together to be the husband you deserve? But only if you stop crying, *cara*, because it is killing me!' he groaned out. 'I need you to love me back, but if you can't I'll spend my life trying to persuade you!' he vowed fiercely.

Maya dashed away the tears that were running down her cheeks. 'Samuele, I love you so much it hurts—'

She didn't get any further than that because he was kissing her and she was kissing him back.

'I love you,' he murmured against her hair when they finally came up for air. 'Have I said that already?'

She pulled back and caught his hand, lifting it to her lips, loving the way his eyes immediately darkened.

'Some things can never be said too often. You have shadows under your eyes, my darling...'

'I spent a very long night realising what a fool I'd been and it was only the fact that I knew you'd hardly had any sleep either that stopped me waking you up... How is Mattio? He sounded pretty upset last night.'

'I think it was just a touch of colic.'

'You're going to make a wonderful mother. Oh, God, Cristiano would have been such a great father. I don't know what I'm doing half the time.'

'You're a great father too, Samuele. There's nobody who will love Mattio more than you. Speaking of which, if I could love you more than I already do, I would,' she whispered huskily as she gazed at him with eyes shining with the strength of her feelings. 'If only Violetta—'

'I have already disposed of that problem—oh, not literally.' He laughed when he saw her face. 'Not that the idea is not tempting,' he added drily. 'But when she heard we were getting married and were applying for full custody, she knew she'd lost because she'd already abandoned Mattio once, so she settled for a final payment instead. Everyone, it turns out, has a price.'

'That must have cost you a lot of money.'

'Money is not important. What is the most important thing is that she has agreed to allow us to formally adopt Mattio so he will officially be our child, and he and our other children will inherit equally.'

'Are we going to have more children?'

'You like the idea?'

She nodded. 'And I will love them all equally,' she promised with damp eyes. 'If they grow up to be like their father, how could I not?'

EPILOGUE

MAYA LAY ON her back on the day bed in the observatory and squirmed languidly, digging her bottom into the soft layer of sheepskins she lay on. 'I wondered what it would be like to make love under the stars.'

'And now you know,' Samuele said smugly. 'I arranged the meteor shower especially for you.'

'Do you think your grandfather ever did this?'

'What, make love under the stars the night before he got married?'

'Well, I quite like the idea of the continuity,' she teased.

'Then I can think of a more pleasant form of continuity. That we spend each of our anniversaries here under the stars making love, though I might not be able to pull off the meteor shower every time.'

She emerged from the long languid kiss with a smile on her lips. 'In six hours and twenty-four minutes, I will be your wife.'

Samuele had wanted it to happen immediately but Maya had insisted she wanted to get married with her family there, which had meant that they'd had to wait a few months until Beatrice's morning sickness had improved enough for her to travel. The timing was perfect: in a dual celebration that morning they had signed the final papers that made them Mattio's adoptive parents.

'Are you all right about it?' she asked.

'Having the woman I love more than life by my side for the rest of our lives? I am *very* all right, *cara*. Come here and I will show you how all right I really am.'

'You've only got six hours and twenty-three minutes left…'

He grinned. 'Six hours will do me just fine.'

* * * * *

Captivated by The Italian's Bride on Paper?
Read Beatrice and Dante's story in
Waking Up in His Royal Bed.

*And why not lose yourself in these other
Kim Lawrence stories?*

A Wedding at the Italian's Demand
A Passionate Night with the Greek
The Spaniard's Surprise Love-Child
Claiming His Unknown Son
Waking Up in His Royal Bed

Available now!

WE HOPE YOU ENJOYED
THIS BOOK FROM

◆HARLEQUIN

PRESENTS

Escape to exotic locations where passion knows no bounds.

Welcome to the glamorous lives of royals and billionaires, where passion knows no bounds. Be swept into a world of luxury, wealth and exotic locations.

8 NEW BOOKS AVAILABLE EVERY MONTH!

HARLEQUIN

***Uplifting or passionate,
heartfelt or thrilling—
Harlequin has your
happily-ever-after.***

With a wide range of romance series that each
offer new books every month, you are sure to
find the satisfying escape you deserve.

Look for all Harlequin series new releases on the *last Tuesday* of each month in stores and online!

Harlequin.com

#3957 BOUND BY HER SHOCKING SECRET
by Abby Green

It takes all of Mia's courage to tell tycoon Daniel about their daughter. Though tragedy tore them apart, he deserves to know he's a father. But accepting his proposal? That will require something far more extraordinary...

#3958 CONFESSIONS OF HIS CHRISTMAS HOUSEKEEPER
by Sharon Kendrick

Stunned when an accident leaves her estranged husband, Giacomo, unable to remember their year-long marriage, Louise becomes his temporary housekeeper. She'll spend Christmas helping him regain his memory. But dare she confess the explosive feelings she still has for him?

#3959 UNWRAPPED BY HER ITALIAN BOSS
Christmas with a Billionaire
by Michelle Smart

After a rocky first impression, innocent Meredith's got a lot to prove to her new billionaire boss, Giovanni! He's trusting her to make his opulent train's maiden voyage a success. Trusting herself around him? That's another challenge entirely...

#3960 THE BILLIONAIRE'S PROPOSITION IN PARIS
Secrets of Billionaire Siblings
by Heidi Rice

By hiring event planner Katherine and inviting her to a lavish Paris ball, Connall plans to find out all he needs to take revenge on her half brother. He's not counting on their ever-building electricity to bring him to his knees!

HPCNMRB1021

"I know how important this maiden voyage is, so I'll give it my
best shot."

What choice did Meredith have? Accept the last-minute second-
ment or lose her job. Those were the only choices. If she lost her
job, what would happen to her? She'd be forced to return to England
while she sought another job. Forced to live in the bleak, unhappy
home of her childhood. All the joy and light she'd experienced these
past three years would be gone, and she'd return to gray.

"What role do you play in it all?" she asked into the silence.

He raised a thick black eyebrow.

"Are you part of Cannavaro Travel?" she queried. "Sorry, my
mind went blank when we were introduced."

The other eyebrow rose.

A tiny dart of amusement at his expression—it was definitely
the expression of someone indignantly thinking, *How can you not
know who I am?*—cut through Merry's guilt and anguish. The guilt
came from having spent two months praying for the forthcoming
trip home to be canceled. The anguish came from her having to be
the one to do it, and with just two days' notice. The early Christmas
dinner her sister-in-law had spent weeks and weeks planning had all
been for nothing. The only good thing she had to hold on to was that
she hadn't clobbered an actual guest with the Christmas tree.

Although, judging by the cut of his suit, Cheekbones was on a huge salary and so must be high up in Cannavaro Travel, and all the signs were that he had an ego to match that salary.

She relaxed her chest with an exhale. "Your role?" she asked again.

Dark blue eyes glittered. Tingles laced her spine and spread through her skin.

Cheekbones folded his hands together on the table. "My role...? Think of me as the boss."

His deep, musical accent set more tingles off in her. Crossing her legs, thankful that she'd come to her senses before mouthing off about being forced into a temporary job she'd rather eat fetid fruit than do, Merry made a mark in her notebook. "I report to you?"

"Sì."

"Are you going on the train ride?"

Strong nostrils flared with distaste. "It is no 'train ride,' lady."

"You know what I mean." She laughed. She couldn't help it. Something about his presence unnerved her. Greek-god looks clashing with a glacial demeanor, warmed up again by the sexiest Italian accent she'd ever heard.

"I know what you mean, and *sì*, I will be on the voyage."

Unnerved further by the swoop of her belly at this, she made another nonsense mark in her book before looking back up at him and smiling ruefully. "In that case, I should confess that I didn't catch your name. I'm Merry," she added, so he wouldn't have any excuse to keep addressing her as "lady."

His fingers drummed on the table. "I know your name, lady. I pay attention."

For some unfathomable reason, this tickled her. "Well done. Go to the top of the class. And your name?"

"Giovanni Cannavaro."

All the blood in Merry's head pooled down to her feet in one strong gush.

Don't miss
Unwrapped by Her Italian Boss.
Available November 2021 wherever
Harlequin Presents books and ebooks are sold.

Harlequin.com